the MAGE'S MAID

FINLEY FENN

The Mage's Maid

info@finleyfenn.com

Cover design by Sylvia at The Book Brander
Proofreading by Emmy from @brabedrebelt

Sign up at www.finleyfenn.com for bonus stories and epilogues, delicious artwork, complete content guidance, news about upcoming books, and more!

ALSO BY FINLEY FENN

THE MAGES

The Mage's Maid

The Mage's Match

The Mage's Master

The Mage's Groom (Bonus Story)

ORC SWORN

The Lady and the Orc

The Heiress and the Orc

The Librarian and the Orc

The Duchess and the Orc

The Midwife and the Orc

The Maid and the Orcs

The Governess and the Orc

The Beauty and the Orcs

The Widow and the Orcs

The Artist and the Orc

Offered by the Orc

Tryggred by the Orc

Yuled by the Orcs

Tales of Orc Sworn

ORC FORGED

The Sins of the Orc

The Fall of the Orc

1

en like Mikkal Mastersson were supposed to get over their house girls.

Gods knew, Mik had tried. It had been five years, probably, since he'd started fucking around, seeing what else was on offer. And for a tall, decent-looking air-mage like him, who just last year had inherited his late father's lands and title, there was a hell of a lot on offer.

But still, Mik kept coming back to Kay.

He could hear his footsteps quickening, the sound echoing off the high-ceilinged hallway, as he made his way to the manor's north wing. To his rooms, which were situated rather closer to the servants' quarters than anyone else's, but there was a reason for that. Just as there was a reason why the rooms were well away from his mother's and sister's, and had a hefty lock installed on the main door.

And that reason—Mik stepped inside, let out a slow breath—was here. Kay.

She was standing by the crackling fireplace, with her back to the door, dressed in her usual black-and-white maid's uniform. There was a dusting cloth on the mantel, sliding itself back and forth, and across the room a fluffy feather duster was sweeping over the polished wood of his bed's huge headboard, making little swirling loops as it went.

There was no indication that Kay was responsible for that—there never was—and that was because Kay was without question the best maid-mage Mik had ever met. Technically an earth-mage, but trained to specialize in light textiles and brushes, and to use them to ensure their employers' homes were spotlessly and effortlessly clean.

Maid-mages were very fashionable these days, and in very high demand, but Miss Kay Courser had worked at Ryning Manor for upwards of twelve years, without complaint. Because—Mik swallowed hard, his eyes running up and down her back—she was *his*.

"Kay," he said, his voice already husky, and slowly she turned to face him. Her tall form ramrod straight, her blonde head held high, her large grey eyes unreadable. Lovely as ever, his Kay, but—

"Lord Ryning," she said, her voice low and smooth, with perhaps a touch of reproach in it. "You've finally returned."

Mik blinked, both at her tone, and the irrational surge of guilt in his gut. And in two loping steps, he was there, pulling Kay's stiff body close into his arms, and running his hands firm and reassuring down her back.

"Don't you 'Lord Ryning' me, love," he murmured against her hair, as he inhaled the heady scent of her, and stroked his hands lower, over the delectable curve of her arse. "Gods, I've missed you."

Kay's own hands slid carefully around Mik's shoulders, but there was an odd hesitation in her fingers, an unsteady hitch in her breath against his neck. "You could have come home," she said. "Or written."

Mik's guilt surged again, but he tamped it down, kept his hands sliding hungry up and down Kay's back through her uniform. "It's been really busy," he replied. "Lots going on. Assignments, new training, a bunch of Coven missions."

But it sounded like an empty excuse, and perhaps it was, because the Coven's Manor for Magical Advancement—the most prestigious magical facility in Vakra, and Mik's full-time employer for the past five years—was only an afternoon's ride away from Ryning Manor, on a good horse. And Mik had several good horses, Mik's job was always busy, and Mik always came home anyway, at least twice a month. To deal with the increasing demands of his new estate, to help his farmers with their fields, to see his mother and his little sister Lea.

And, always, to see Kay.

"You could have written," Kay said again, into his neck, and again that guilt lurched, this time laced with a twinge of irritation. Mik couldn't write Kay, and she knew that very well. Landed lords did not write letters to their housemaids, and if ever they did, it would be an order of some sort, and not an estimated date of one's arrival home, because what if such a letter were intercepted? By the other servants, one's colleagues, one's *mother*?

"It was really busy," he said again, but it sounded even emptier than before, and abruptly Kay pulled back from him, her intent grey eyes meeting his. Searching his, looking for truth, and Mik winced, even as his gaze slid away, to the safety of her still-twirling feather duster.

And the truth was, he *had* been busy—but it hadn't been work keeping him from home. It had been Ilsa, a buxom, beautiful, dark-haired water-mage at Coven Manor. A girl who was well-born, and well-to-do, and proper partner material.

And these days, Mik needed to be looking at proper possibilities. Needed to find someone who could ultimately become a real lord's wife, provide real lord's heirs, and run a real lord's household. And far more difficult, he needed to find a girl who could do all that, while also keeping Mik's interest, and conquering the dismissive, ever-encroaching apathy that always seemed to plague his intimate relations.

Except, of course, here.

"You were gone for two *months*, Mik," Kay's wavering voice said. "With no word, not even to your mother, or Lea, or Scullen. Smit's fields desperately need water, and Lea sent you a letter every single week with no reply, and it was my *birthday*, and—"

Damn it. Kay's birthday. Mik grimaced, his eyes flicking back to hers, catching on the unsettling misery in them. Kay rarely made demands of him like this—it was one of the many things he liked about her—but her family had all been dead for years, so Mik had always tried to do something special for her birthday. And the thought of her spending this year's sitting alone in the servants' quarters, waiting in vain for him to come home, was doing strange things in the pit of his stomach.

"I did buy you those extra painting supplies before I left, last time," he said, but that was a flimsy excuse too, and Kay's gaze pulled away, her eyes blinking hard. Because Mik always bought Kay supplies. He knew how much she loved her little painting hobby, how it occupied every last minute of her limited spare time. And he'd supported her in it for years, shelling out for a steady stream of expensive classes and tutors and books and paints and brushes, and he'd even arranged to create a little private studio space for her, in one of the unused rooms on the manor's top floor.

And, Mik had always thought, it had been plenty. It had been far more than any other employer would have ever given any other housemaid. And Kay was lucky she had her maid-mage status to mark her as special among the other servants, or else Mik's rampant generosity would have likely come back to bite him in the arse years ago.

But right now Kay's lovely face was still looking away from him, her eyes bright with tears, and Mik felt his resolve floundering, the regret rising to fill its place. "Look, love, I'm sorry I missed your birthday," he said, and he meant it. "Tell me what you'd like for a belated gift, and I'll have it for you tomorrow. Walrus-whisker brushes, perhaps? A long-lost thousand-year-old instructional book? Crushed red beetles from across the ocean?"

He was teasing now, and he could see the unwilling flare of warmth cross Kay's eyes. He always knew how to cajole her, how to bring up that smile, and he kept at it, raising a suggestive hand, wiggling his fingers, and then drawing just enough magic to blow a sharp, warm gust of wind toward her face. Blowing the silly maid's cap off her head, and halfway across the room—but just before it hit the floor, her twirling feather duster soared to catch it, and flew back over to throw it straight in Mik's face.

Mik blew the cap aside, and grinned at Kay—that was more like it—and then relaxed all over when she smiled back. Not with her usual warm ease, but close, and closer still when Mik's hand caught her chin, tilting it up, so he could blow out another puff of wind at her. Stronger this time, whipping out wisps of her blonde waves from her tight bun, and making her eyes flutter with undeniable hunger.

"You want to do this the easy way, love?" Mik murmured, soft, as his other hand traced down her cheek. "Or the hard way?"

Kay's eyes fluttered again, and her throat spasmed, her chest heaving against him. "The hard way," she whispered. "If you want."

Fuck, yes, of course Mik wanted, but he held his straining body still, and searched her still-bright eyes. "You're sure?" he whispered. "We can do it sweet. Or you can kick my delinquent arse out altogether, if you like."

Kay's smile twitched up again, showing the dimple in her cheek this time, and she gave a regal little toss of her blonde head. "No," she said. "I'd far rather make you pay for your sins, arsehole. I mean"—she gave a sly, rather sharp-toothed smile—"your lordship."

Gods. A low growl burned from Mik's throat, and his hands settled hungry and proprietary to the front of Kay's uniform, curving over the swell of her breasts. "Then it's time to start serving your lord, sweetheart," he murmured, as he tilted his head, cast his usual sound-suppressing spell on the air around them. "On your knees, to start. And don't you *dare* stop cleaning."

He could feel the hunger tremble down Kay's body, her cheeks heating, her eyes sparking with warmth. And without warning, she took a quick, graceful step back from him, and raised her hand, and—Mik moaned, even as he recoiled—slapped him hard across the face.

"No, you entitled arrogant *prig*," she breathed. "You're my employer, not my john. And I will *never* get on my knees for the likes of you."

Fuck, it had been a long time, and Mik's replying groan felt more like a shudder, ripping itself through his skin. He was already rock-hard, his dick thrusting almost painfully against his close-fitting trousers, and he took a strong, swift step back toward her, and circled his hands tight around both her wrists.

"You don't get to choose, sweetheart," he said, and followed the words with another hard gust of air, blowing straight in her face, whipping more hair out of her tight bun. "I'm the lord, you're the servant. Get the *fuck* on your knees."

But this was where the magic came in, where the thrill of the game came in, because with a single, disdainful glance of Kay's grey eyes, Mik's waistcoat rapidly unbuttoned itself, and flew up from behind to cover his face. Pressing its thick wool fabric tight and suffocating against his mouth and nose, and Mik had to release Kay's wrists to grasp for it, and yank it off, and thrust it away behind him.

"Disrespectful wench," he growled, as he advanced closer to her, and threw up an air-shield behind her, to keep her from backing away. "Apologize. On your knees, before I *make* you."

Kay's mouth betrayed a high-pitched gasp, but with another disdainful, purposeful look from her eyes, Mik felt his thick necktie jerk backwards, hard, the pain almost eye-watering as he staggered to catch his footing. And once he was steady and breathing again, he scrabbled to yank the tie off, hurling it with force behind him, while Kay just watched, with cool amusement in her grey eyes.

"Are you recovered, my lord?" she said, crisp and biting, and this time when Mik stalked forward, his air-shield came close behind him, keeping his momentum. Even as he felt both his shirt and trousers tugging backwards too, his trousers rubbing extra hard against his swollen groin, gods *curse* the wench.

"On your *knees*," he bit out. "*Now.*"

But Kay's only reply was a saucy tilt of her head, an angling of her eyes toward the locked bottom drawer of his heavy wooden wardrobe. And as Mik gasped, the lock clicked itself open, the drawer snapped out, and a long, thick rope slowly uncoiled itself, and slithered itself over toward him, not unlike a huge, horrifying serpent.

Mik threw up an air-shield with a wave of his hand, blocking the rope-serpent's path—but it only slithered down and sideways and back again, searching for a way around. Because while Mik could cast a good impenetrable air-shield, he'd never been able to manage a full protective circle, and Kay knew that, giving a cold, hard smile as her serpent found the edge, and lunged itself around it, straight toward Mik's face.

Within a breath, the rope was curling around Mik's neck, close and constricting, and his hands frantically grasped for it, to no avail. Instead, it only wound itself around again, dragging him backwards, pinning him flat up against his own air-shield still behind him. And now it was Kay advancing toward him, tall and smug and smiling, looking every bit the dangerous powerful witch, out on the hunt for blood.

"That's better," she murmured, as the rope wound a little tighter, scraping against the tender skin of Mik's neck. Not tight enough to be truly painful or dangerous, but certainly enough to prevent Mik's moving, his breath coming sharp and ragged as Kay put a single finger to his chin.

"What do you say now, your lordship?" she asked. "Will you apologize for attempting to defile such an innocent, loyal servant?"

Mik barked a hoarse laugh, even as he kicked up another flare of air, this time directly under Kay's long, voluminous skirts. Making them blow upwards with satisfying force, enough to show the pale skin of her bare thighs and hips, and just a hint of the coarse hair at her groin.

"Innocent, my arse," he ground out, as Kay thrust her skirts down again, her cheeks now a gratifying shade of pink. "Walking around all day without a stitch of anything on underneath, just waiting for your lord to come and give you what you deserve."

Kay's throat let out a rather unladylike growl, and the rope around Mik's neck jerked backwards, hard. "As your loyal subject," she hissed, "I deserve your kindness, and your benevolence. I deserve more than casual treatment as a tawdry disposable *plaything* for your entitled lordship's casual *enjoyment!*"

Her voice cracked slightly on the words, making Mik blink, his throat swallowing hard against the ropes—and for an instant Kay's eyes squeezed shut, her breath exhaling harsh. "And," she continued, her voice wavering, "you're simply far too deep up your own tight royal arse to admit what a lustful, licentious lech you are. Coveting chaste, innocent maidens like you do."

Mik felt himself exhale—that was better, that was the game—and he tried for a disdainful look of his own, a curl of his lip. "You think I covet a servant like *you*?" he asked, as coolly as he could. "A disobedient, disrespectful cleaning maid? That's rubbish, wench."

"Rubbish, is it?" Kay snapped back, and with a sharp wave of her hand, the front fall of his trousers swiftly yanked downwards, and—Mik groaned, and heard Kay groan too—thereby freed his swollen, aching dick. Leaving him standing there gasping for air, with a rope circled tight around his neck, and his thick, hard, leaking cock protruding out the front of his trousers.

"That's not for you, wench," he gritted out, but in reply Kay gave a cold, brittle laugh. And as Mik watched, the buttons of her black maid's apron began to slowly, deliberately untwist themselves, opening down her front, one by one.

"You want this, your lordship," she murmured, as the black apron peeled itself off her, revealing the low-cut white chemise beneath. "You want your sweet innocent housemaid, because you're a lying reprobate *rake*."

"I am not," Mik protested, but his mouth was dry, his staring eyes caught on the sight of Kay gracefully stepping out of her black slippers, as the white chemise slowly twirled itself up. And up, and up, Kay raising her arms to let it soar off over her head, and—Mik let out a desperate, ragged gasp—left her standing there naked in the middle of his bedroom.

And fuck, she was gorgeous. Up there with the most beautiful, expensively done-up girls he'd ever had, though maybe that was just his own self-induced bias coming in, after making this one his first, and keeping at it for ten years running. But even objectively, Kay's body was long and supple and smooth, her skin pale and flawless, her bare breasts pert and peaked, just the way he liked. And her hair—Mik nearly choked as it tumbled down over her shoulders—was long and wavy and shining, and made her look like a true goddess, like one of her paintings come to life.

And the goddess was raising an eyebrow, mocking him, because—Mik didn't even need to look down—his bare, exposed cock was wildly twitching, desperately fighting to get closer. Needing her hands, her mouth, her slick silken heat, anything, fuck, *please*.

"What do you say, my lord?" she said, blinking at him under her eyelashes, for all the world suddenly a sweet, innocent, undefiled maiden. And Mik had to try to think, try to remember that there was still a *rope* around his neck, holy mother of the gods.

"I say," he croaked, "you're full of it, wench. You clean my *house*. You're lucky I can even stand to look at you, let alone tolerate your mouth on my dick. Which"—he pulled in more air—"you're going to do *now*. Or else."

"Is that so?" Kay said, raising a curious eyebrow, running a teasing, tantalizing hand down the front of Mik's rumpled shirt, and coming dangerously close to his protruding, still-twitching prick. "Or what, your lordship?"

"Or I make you," Mik growled. "Last warning, wench."

But Kay only smiled, as her finger came down further, and—oh fuck—traced itself slowly, deliberately, down the full length of his trembling shaft. "I don't think so, your lordship," she murmured. "If anything, it's *you* who should be apologizing to *me*. You who should be bending over, and exposing your tight little lordly arse to me. You who should be begging for *my* punishment."

As she spoke, the still-twirling feather duster floated over toward her, and snapped itself into her outstretched, waiting fingers. That damned feather duster, which—Mik swallowed—had a slim, supple switch embedded in the fluffy feathers. And also—Kay spun it in her fingers, so the other end pointed up—a slim, smooth, rounded wooden handle. Which had, indeed, found its way up Mik's tight lordly arse, more than once.

"Like hell, wench," he murmured, but he was eyeing the handle, curse him, considering it. While Kay's eyebrows rose higher, and a flick of her finger sent the feather duster floating downwards, where it started trailing itself up and down the hard length of him, gods damn it.

But no, no, he'd promised his mother he would be down for supper, and that would add a good hour to the proceedings, and Kay very well knew it. And she was distracted, maybe wanting it as much as he did, so Mik closed his eyes, dragged in the magic, deep—

And with a sharp breath, a snap of his hand in the air, the rope flew off his neck, thrust away by two simultaneous soaring air-shields. While another air-shield pressed powerfully down on the top of Kay's head, making her stagger and sink to her knees on the cold tiled floor.

She scrabbled to rise, to bring the rope-serpent back again, but Mik tossed it away across the room, and split his air-shield into two, one pressing down on each of her shoulders. Shoving her down to kneeling, but leaving her head alone, so she could glare and snarl at him, her hands casting spell after useless spell, fighting and failing to get through his shields.

"I warned you, wench," Mik said coolly, as he came a deliberate step closer, his swollen, twitching prick only a handsbreadth from her reddened, gasping face. "You're going to apologize for your disrespect, and you're going to do it thoroughly. Open up."

Kay didn't, of course, so Mik put a hand to her mouth, and roughly tugged it open. Thrusting two fingers deep inside, while his other hand reached back to grasp a handful of her golden hair, tilting her head up, making her look at him. "That's more like it," he drawled. "You like that?"

She couldn't speak, of course, not with his fingers delving

like that against her throat—but he could see her nod, barely imperceptible. Saying yes, because she always wanted this, needed this, just as much as he did.

So Mik took his time pulling her lower jaw down, opening up her mouth. And then, his breaths heaving, eyes staring at the sight, he leaned forward, and slowly, finally—*finally*—slid his cock between her lips, and deep into her hot, clenching throat.

Kay was fighting not to gag—she'd taught herself that just for him, years ago—and Mik kept staring, gasping as he felt the impossibly tight slickness of her mouth, her convulsing throat, encasing him in hot, glorious heat. She was one of the few girls he'd had who could take him all the way, let alone keep him there like that, and Mik revelled in the sight of it, the feel of it, his golden goddess with his dick buried deep down her throat, *fuck*.

He could feel her starting to struggle, her breath dragging harsh through her nose—and then there were teeth, sharp, scraping against the base of him. Meaning that she was done, for now, and Mik yanked himself out, tried to glare down at her as he grasped his shaft, and then slapped its thick length across her face, hard.

"Disobedient wench," he hissed, making her blink up at him, her face now bright red, and covered with a sheen of sweat. "When I deign to give you your lordship's dick, you take it properly. The way I taught you."

Kay desperately nodded, her breath heaving, and Mik gave a dark, satisfied smile as he sank himself back into her mouth, all the way, driving back deep against her clenching, convulsing throat. "You're out of practice, wench," he gasped. "You need to be trained again to please your lord. Beg me to train you."

Kay couldn't, of course, with his dick in her mouth, but she made an unintelligible noise, and Mik gave another dark smile, bearing down deeper. "That's it," he murmured. "Beg me again."

He was pulling her hair back still, but she wasn't begging this time, just blinking and glaring and gasping, her hands now fluttering at his still-clothed thighs. So Mik pulled back, pulled out, slapped her with his prick again, making her hiss as her head snapped sideways at the impact—*fuck*, the *sight* of that— and then he slammed himself back in, hard, and out again, and back in.

"This is what you get," he rasped, as he gouged himself into her throat, again and again. "You forget how to suck me properly, I'm going to use your throat so hard you won't be able to speak for a fucking *week*—"

Kay was groaning around him, in it just as much as he was, the saliva dripping wet and slick now, pooling down her chin as he slammed in and out and in again. Using her, taking her, showing her where she belonged, what was *his*—

Until she shoved him away, hard, not with her hands, but with her magic. Holding him back by the trousers, but she wasn't looking at him, her golden head was sideways and down, the back of her hand wiping against her swollen lips.

Maybe Mik should have stopped there, but the towering demanding craving was breathtakingly strong. And when he reached and snapped Kay's chin up, her eyes were sparkling, and with another wave of her hand, she thrust him away, across the room.

There was an instant's choked silence, hanging hungry and desperate in the air between them—and suddenly Kay rushed at him, or maybe he'd rushed at her, because they were both in the middle of the room again, hands grabbing and shoving and pulling, gripping on sweaty skin. Mik's shirt flying off, his trousers ripping into pieces as they flew back behind him, and he was naked and she was naked and he threw her onto the bed, even as she dragged him after her, her fingernails ripping painful into his back.

"Just fuck me, Mik," she gasped, breathless, into his mouth, which was ravaging hers so hard their teeth smashed together. "Please, my lord, *please.*"

Mik was already between her thighs, yanking her closer, her arse halfway off the bed, her legs spreading wide, showing him the quivering hungry open heat between them—and Mik choked out a curse, or maybe a prayer, as he sank himself deep inside. Hard and hot and furious, and Kay screeched and writhed beneath him, tight and close and clenching all around him, *his*, oh gods, oh fuck, have *mercy.*

"You like that, wench," he gasped, as he slammed inside, deeper and harder with every thrust. "You want your lord, you want me, you want *me.*"

Kay moaned and sputtered and desperately nodded, her hands tangling in his hair as she dragged him down closer, yanked his mouth back to hers. "Yes," she breathed, "yes, fuck, Mik, please, *please—*"

Mik was so close he could taste it, his eyes rolling back, his groin pulling up tight—when suddenly under him Kay stilled, one hand still clenched in his hair, the other fluttering against his lips. "The spell," she gasped, "to prevent pregnancy, I had it taken off—"

It took far too long for Mik to comprehend that, even as his body teetered closer, closer to the edge—and just in time he yanked himself out of her, and sprayed out his release. Spurting white and sticky all over Kay's heaving belly and breasts, as the pleasure rolled and surged through him, pounding again and again and again, glory so breathtaking it was *life.*

"Fuck," Mik gasped, blinking down at the sight of Kay beneath him, spread-eagled and debauched, her face flushed, her eyes bright. Her breath heaving just as hard as his, and Mik drank in the sight of that, her breasts shuddering, spattered with his spunk, *fuck.*

"Gods damn it, Kay," he breathed, as he dropped his shaky body down onto the bed beside her. "*Fuck.* That's what two months does to a guy."

He'd meant it to be a joke, but a glance sideways toward Kay showed her still breathing hard, her eyes blinking at the ceiling. "Oh, come now, Mik," she said, her voice hoarse. "It's not like you were celibate for two whole months, were you?"

Mik let out a slow breath, and carefully turned himself to face her on the bed. "Were *you*?" he heard his traitorous voice ask, and Kay's hands rose to her face, her palms pressing hard against her eyes.

"Yes," she said, sounding strangely weary. "I always am, Mik."

Something odd lurched up in Mik's throat, but he swallowed it back, took a breath. "Thank you," he murmured, though the words sounded inadequate, and maybe even shameful. Because he knew—and Kay knew, too—that if she were to fuck someone else, even kiss or touch someone else, Mik would lose his shit.

Kay didn't reply, didn't look at him, and Mik's thoughts faltered, his eyes darting away for something, anything—and found it in Kay's dusting cloth, still sliding back and forth across the fireplace mantel. Because he'd told her not to stop cleaning in that, and so of course she hadn't, brilliant snarky wench that she was.

"You can stop cleaning now, love," he said, tracing a careful hand against the part of her waist that he hadn't made a mess of, and her breath heaved in, and out again, as she raised her hand, and flew the cloth over toward them. Where it promptly began wiping up the mess on her skin, an action that was both regrettable and welcome, since once it was done, Mik could pull her warm body close, circle his arm over her, run his hand smooth and reassuring up her still-sticky flank.

"You're brilliant, my lovely Kay," he murmured, against her hair. "Better than anyone else. You know that."

Kay twitched a tight little nod, blinking up toward the ceiling, and Mik studied her, his eyes narrowing. She was usually far more receptive to him afterwards, would usually have been snuggling herself all up against him, and likely teasing that she could have made very good use of the feather duster, whether he'd allowed it or not.

But there was only this stilted silence, her eyes still staring straight up, and Mik's gaze lingered there, and then down to where he'd made that mess on her skin. And that had been strange, exceptionally strange in fact, because she'd been on that spell for years and years, ever since an early and unfortunate mistake had ended with her at an expensive healer's for a week, and with Mik getting a good earful from his furious father.

"So why did you take off the spell?" he asked, carefully, even as he kept his hand sliding easy and gentle on her skin. "Shouldn't we have talked about that first?"

He could see Kay's throat swallowing, her jaw clenching tight. "Well, shouldn't we have also talked about you not coming home for two whole months?"

Mik squeezed his eyes shut, and made himself bite back the rising, overpowering urge to tell her to fuck off, and leave it alone. She was entitled to how she felt, he'd missed her birthday, and she'd also just given him that spectacular, mind-melting fuck, so much better than anything else he'd had otherwise these past two months.

"I'm sorry, love," he said, with a sigh. "Next time, I'll make sure you know."

It was a concession, a real one, but if Mik expected it to

help, it didn't. Instead, it only seemed to make Kay's eyes blink harder, her hand rubbing against her pink, swollen lips.

"It was another girl, wasn't it?" she whispered. "A girl you were serious about."

Mik briefly thought about lying, but Kay didn't deserve that, and he sighed again, kept his hand sliding on her skin. "Yeah," he said. "But it didn't work out."

He wasn't about to get into why, not with her—one couldn't exactly tell one's housemaid that a proper titled girl was boring as shit, compared to her. But too late, he realized that he should have said something, anything, because that was a single glistening tear, streaking down Kay's cheek. And worse still, a quiet little sniff from her nose, and oh gods, she was *crying*, and Mik hated it when girls cried—

"Look, Kay, you know what's expected of me," he told her, harsher than he should have, but it had to be said. "I need to find a proper wife to help run the estate, to give me heirs. Somebody who society will accept, who can stand in for me when I need it, and make sure Mother and Lea are taken care of, if anything ever happens to me. And I'm sorry, Kay, but that woman can't be you."

Kay nodded fervently toward the ceiling, even as another tear streaked from her eye, down onto Mik's bed. Still crying, he'd made his Kay *cry*. And suddenly he just felt utterly wretched, and he pulled himself up a little, so he could wipe the wetness away from her cheeks.

"But I still adore you, Kay," he said, softer now. "You know I do. All right?"

Kay kept nodding, still not looking at him, and he could hear her swallow, hard. "I know, Mik," she whispered. "Gods, I know. I adore you, too. And that's why"—she swallowed again—"I'm leaving."

2

Kay was leaving.

Mik gaped at her, at those truly appalling words, and suddenly his heart was thudding, fighting to punch its way out of his chest. "What?!" he heard himself say, in a voice that wasn't his. "You can't *leave!*"

But Kay abruptly sat up, pulling away from him, pressing her palms to her eyes. "Yes, Mik, I can," she croaked. "I'm not contracted here in any way. I'm your *employee*, here of my own free will. And that means"—she dropped her hands, looked at him over her shoulder with eyes that were suddenly tired, miserable—"I can leave. Which I will. Next week."

Next *week*?! Mik's mouth was hanging open, his heart still thundering against his ribcage, and he pulled himself up beside her, gave his head a hard shake. "But you like it here!" he protested, his voice still too high-pitched. "You have a good job here. A *great* job, with good pay, and good benefits!"

Kay shot him a sharp, disbelieving look, and Mik grimaced, even as he reached for her hand, closed it in both of his. "You can't just *leave*, Kay," he said. "What would you even do?"

Kay gave him another sharp look, almost pained this time.

"I know this may come as a surprise to you, Mik," she replied, "but servants like me command a premium. I could work in any other noble house in Vakra and make twice the salary I do here. The only reason I've stayed this long"—she took a wavering breath—"is the *benefits*, Mik."

Mik recoiled backwards, almost like when she'd slapped him earlier. "So that's what you're doing, then?" he demanded. "You got a better offer somewhere else? With better *benefits*?"

Kay winced, and rubbed at her eyes again. "No, Mik, there aren't better benefits than you, all right? I'm going"—she drew in a heavy, shaky breath—"I'm going to move out, and open my own studio. As an artist."

Her own studio. An artist. Mik was staring again, his hands gone slack against hers, and he couldn't seem to pull that together, or make sense of it. An artist. Kay wasn't a real artist, she was a *housemaid*, she was *his*—

"Do you," he began, his voice rough. "You think you can— actually make a living at that? You're not *really* an artist, Kay, you're just—"

He bit back the words, far too late, because Kay's lovely face had briefly crumpled, into something ugly and sad, before it turned abruptly away from him. "I know you may not see me as a real artist, Mik," her thick voice said, "but plenty of other people do. I've turned down multiple commissions this year, three just this month, one who offered to take me to the capital, all expenses paid, to do a sitting there. And I've *told* you I get commissions, Mik, I've told you people like my work, and it's like you're not even listening to a single word I say."

Mik felt rooted to the bed, to the house, the world, to the stillness of her golden head, still looking away from him. "It's like—you'll never get past this vision of me as your housemaid," she continued, her voice harder, bitter. "As your—*harlot*. And housemaid harlots aren't real people, so they can't actually be good at other things, can they?"

The words felt like daggers, stabbing one after the other into Mik's gut, and he couldn't seem to speak. Could only grip his hands against her waist, sink his head to her stiff shoulder, blink his eyes as hard as he could. "For fuck's sakes, Kay," he breathed, choked, into her skin. "Of course you're a real person. You"—he hauled in a breath—"you've been my best friend, my best girl, for as long as I've known you. For almost half my life. I think about you every fucking *day*."

He could feel Kay wilting slightly against him, and he slid his arms around her, pulled her closer. "Why?" he asked, hoarse. "Why now? Because I was away for so long?"

Her shoulder jerked a shrug against him, her face still turned purposely away. "Because," she said, her voice cracking, "two weeks ago, I had my twenty-sixth birthday. And I was always sure by the time I was twenty-five, I would have my own life, my own family. But it hasn't happened, and I think I finally realized"—her whole body shuddered—"that as long as I stay here, it never will."

Mik still couldn't seem to find words, and he grasped for coherence, for truth. "But I—I thought you liked it here. In general. Not just—the *benefits*."

Kay shrugged again, and her hands snapped up the abandoned feather duster from the floor, absently smoothing the feathers with her fingers. "I do," she said, looking down toward it. "Your mother and Lea are lovely to me, I get along with the other servants, I know all your tenants and labourers. But I'm still a servant here, Mik. I'm *paid* to clean your house. I have to wear a uniform and sleep in a room with three other people and wake up before dawn and report to your mother whenever I so much as want to take a walk."

Mik couldn't speak at all now, just blinking at her blonde head, and he felt her shoulders rise, and fall. "And I want a family," she added, quieter. "It's been so many years since I had one, and I *need* it, Mik, so much it hurts. And I don't want that one time"—her voice caught—"to be the one chance I had at it. But as long as I'm here it won't happen, you know it won't, because I clean your house. And that means I'm good enough to fuck on the sly, good enough to have your way with, but not good enough to have your child. Whether I'm supposedly your best girl, or not."

The last of it came out choked, angry, and Mik desperately wanted to deny it. But his own thoughtless actions of a quarter-hour ago would have lain waste to the lie, and what if she'd done that as some kind of fucked-up test, gods damn her, damn *him*.

But Mik still wasn't speaking, because maybe there was nothing else to say, and Kay jolted up to her feet, and away from him. Lurching unsteadily toward her uniform, still neatly draped over the chair where she'd left it, and even as Mik opened his mouth to protest, her white chemise rose up and twirled down over her head, concealing her naked body from his view. And then the black apron, buttoning itself up, and even her hair was twisting neatly up onto her head, fastening itself into its tight bun without even a twitch of her fingers.

"I'm sorry for ruining your trousers," she said, formally, over her shoulder, as she carefully placed the feather duster on the mantel. "If you leave them in the bottom of your wardrobe, I'll have them mended for you."

With that, she strode toward the door, and unlocked it with a single wave of her hand. She was leaving, his Kay was *leaving*, like this—and far too late Mik's coherence snapped back into place, just in time to throw up his strongest air-shield, right between her and the door.

"Kay," he said to her back, as he stumbled up to his feet. "Don't leave like this. We can talk about this. Work something out. All right?"

But Kay shook her head, and her hand spread flat against Mik's air-shield, fingers wide. "You had your chance to talk," she said, quiet. "And you told me I wasn't a real artist, that I can't have your child, and that you need to find a proper woman who can be a proper wife to you. And that woman isn't me. I don't know what else you *want* from me, Mik."

Mik stared at her, struggling for words, for sanity, and Kay put her other hand up to his air-shield, still blocking her in. "Please, Mik," she whispered. "I need to go."

But Mik didn't drop the shield—she couldn't leave like this, she *couldn't*—and finally she turned to look at him, her lovely face streaked with tears. "Let me go, Mik," she said. "Please. We're done."

But Mik's head was shaking, he couldn't, she couldn't, or so he thought—but as he stared, her hands on his shield spread wide, and somehow—pushed. Pushed herself through it, or pushed the shield behind her, and his housemaid could break his best *air-shield*, what the *fuck*—

"Goodbye, Mik," Kay said, and she stepped outside, and shut the door behind her.

3

It was a good half-hour before Mik finally made it down to supper.

He'd done his damnedest to pull himself together, both physically and otherwise, but it had taken far too long, and far too much effort. And though he'd succeeded in properly dressing, and covering the new rope burns on his neck with a high-necked collar, as he descended the stairs into the dining room he still felt thoroughly stunned, and unsettled, and on edge.

Kay was *leaving*. And she couldn't leave, it had to be some kind of massive miscommunication... right? Mik just needed to talk to her, make her properly understand, cajole and tease her until she came around again.

But when he stepped into the dining room, where his mother and his little sister Lea were already seated, his steps faltered, his hands clenching to fists. Because Kay was *here*, she was serving his mother a plate of dinner, and her golden head was bowed, her eyes not even glancing up to where Mik was standing in the doorway.

But she had to walk past him to go back to the kitchen, so

Mik stood there in the doorway, holding his grim eyes on hers. Waiting, waiting for her to look up as she approached—but she didn't. Only murmured, "Excuse me, my lord," as she edged by him, her eyes carefully on the floor.

It only added to the uneasy frustration building in Mik's gut, and he stalked over to the table, and yanked out his usual chair at the head, with his mother and Lea on either side. Lea looking up at him with warmth in her sparkling eyes, and his mother's grey-streaked head tilting with something quieter, more measured.

Mik attempted a smile toward them as he sank into his chair, and spread the napkin on his lap. He truly loved his mother and Lea, and always had. His mother was kind and generous, and since she'd been several decades younger—and much less self-destructively inclined—than his fast-living father, she had been a very real and supportive presence in his life growing up. She had also stood between Mik and his enraged father on too many occasions to count, and even now it was a shared camaraderie between them, that they'd both survived him, and come out intact on the other side.

And Lea—Mik's smile at her almost felt genuine—was a sweet, infuriating delight, wrapped in a compact, energetic, black-haired form that almost never stopped talking. She was only thirteen, less than half Mik's age, and some days Mik felt more like her father than his own father had ever been.

"You're late," Lea pronounced at him. "Again. What were you doing up there in your room all alone, working *again*?"

At that most inopportune time, Kay strode back through the door, this time carrying Mik's plate. And Mik felt his face heating, his unease surging again, as he glanced up at her distant, lowered eyes.

"Thank you," he murmured, but there still wasn't the slightest response, and he had to force his gaze back to Lea, who was eyeing him expectantly. "Just getting some much needed recovery time," he told her, perhaps for Kay's benefit, but she was already striding away again, her back ramrod straight. "A guy needs a break once in a while."

"All too true," Lea said, with a dark look in his direction. "You work way too much, Mik. Eight letters you didn't return. *Eight.*"

"I know," Mik replied, and the guilt bubbled up again, clamouring with the rest of the mess in his gut. "It's been a ridiculous few weeks, munchkin. I'll do better next time, I promise. I'll send extra-long missives breaking out every tedious detail of my excessively tedious days."

"You better," Lea snapped, though she looked slightly mollified, and took a large bite of her supper. "Better yet, you'll just quit that slog already. You're a lord now, Mik, why do you have to work your tail off like you do? We don't need the money that badly anymore, do we?"

Kay had come back into the room as Lea spoke, and Mik's traitorous gaze followed her again, even as his floundering thoughts searched for an answer. He liked his work at Coven Manor, yes, but it was true that their finances were much improved these days, and all the time away was impacting his responsibilities here. But he couldn't come back here for good, not until he'd locked down that wife, because—Kay's hand trembled slightly as she filled his mother's wine glass—if he was here, having Kay every day, he'd probably give up on the whole damned idea altogether.

"I know I won't be staying there long-term," he said carefully, still eyeing Kay, "but there are still a few things I need to wrap up. When I'm ready to quit, you'll be the first to know."

Lea looked pleased at that, and tucked into her supper with gusto. While Kay walked out again, still without a single glance in Mik's direction, and when Mik frowned back at the table, he found his mother still watching him, her head thoughtfully tilted.

"Why do you have Kay serving?" he asked her, before he could stop herself. "That's not her job, is it?"

"Hallum is sick," his mother replied, "and Cook wanted to keep Mel with her to help, since she went overboard in the kitchen, knowing you were home."

Right. Mik dutifully turned his attention to the plate of food before him, and it all did look lovely, roasted fowl and seasoned crisp vegetables and fresh-baked bread. Even so, he wasn't even slightly hungry, not with his stomach still churning painfully in his gut, and he had to make himself take a bite, swallow it down.

"It's delicious," he said stiffly. "Please give Cook and Mel my thanks."

His mother nodded, still studying him as she took a sip of her wine, and Mik turned his attention back to Lea. "I did read all your letters, even if I was horribly neglectful in writing back," he told her. "So was the party at Poole's really that great?"

It was the right question, thankfully, and Lea immediately launched into a litany of comparisons to similar parties, and the people she'd seen there, and how mother had allowed her to have a new dress made just for the occasion. Leaving Mik to nod along, and insert the appropriate comments in the appropriate places, while his thoughts circled, brooded, sank ever deeper into something like misery. Kay was *leaving*.

He made it through most of supper without incident—but then, of course, Kay had to return, to clear away the settings. And she didn't once look at Mik as she took away his mother's, and then Lea's, walking away, away, *leaving*—and when she came for Mik's, it was like the misery had swarmed up into an irrational, unconquerable rage. She was his, she was ignoring him, she couldn't *leave*.

His hand snapped up to grasp her wrist of its own accord, holding her there, and he could feel her freeze, her eyes staring intent at the table. But still not looking at him, and curse him, but Mik drew her down, so her face was close to his. And when her eyes finally darted to his, they were uneasy and almost—afraid.

"Come to my room tonight," he muttered, very quiet, into her ear. "Please."

The colour rose sharply in Kay's cheeks, her eyes blinking back down at the table, and Mik abruptly released her hand. "All right?" he said, out loud, because curse him, that way she had to answer—and she jerked a tight little nod.

"Yes, my lord," she whispered, and then she turned and strode away, leaving Mik's plate and cutlery abandoned where they stood.

When Mik looked back at the table, both his mother and Lea were watching, Lea with open curiosity in her eyes, and he silently cursed himself, and Kay, and this whole ridiculous situation. "She's working on a project for me," he said, as a pathetic explanation. "A painting."

Lea's eyes immediately filled with understanding, and she decisively nodded. "Oh yes, before she goes," she replied. "That makes sense. Though I'm still upset that she's leaving, what if we get some cranky old biddy instead who's no fun, and takes ages to do everything?"

She pouted at Mik, as though it was all his fault, and he swallowed hard, fought through another surge of irrational fury. "So you *knew* Kay was leaving, then?" he asked, as calmly as he could. "Why didn't you mention that in your letters?"

It was fucking ridiculous, really, that Lea had gone on about parties and books and clothes, when she'd known all along that Kay was *leaving*—and Lea shot him an uneasy look, clearly picking up on his displeasure, while across the table their mother cleared her throat. "Kay asked us not to mention it, Mikkal," she said, with a slight warning in her voice, "until she'd had a chance to discuss it with you directly. As you are technically her employer now."

Gods damn his mother, damn Lea, damn Kay for trying to *leave* him. And Mik couldn't seem to stop glaring at the table, clenching his fingers hard against it, and he only distantly noticed when his mother quietly dismissed Lea, promising on Mik's behalf that they would all have a game of cards later.

Lea finally went out, leaving Mik and his mother alone, with Mik still glaring at the table. Feeling his mother still watching him, seeing far too much, like she always did.

"Are you all right, Mikkal?" she asked, into the silence. "You don't seem to be taking this well."

"I don't know what you're talking about," Mik replied, unnecessarily curt, and then inwardly winced as his mother exhaled a heavy sigh.

"I'm talking about Kay," she said pointedly. "As you well know."

Mik shot a swift glance toward the door, but thankfully Lea had closed it, and he sagged back into his chair. "I don't want to talk about it."

He'd never fully admitted about Kay to his mother, but he was well aware that she knew, and maybe even Lea did, too. It was impossible not to, living in the same house the way they did—and also, when one's younger self had gotten said housemaid pregnant, years before. But Mik had always strived to be discreet, to not bring shame on himself or Kay or his family, and that meant they didn't talk about it, ever. Men like him were supposed to get over their house girls.

"Mikkal," his mother said, with a trace of warning in her voice. "She's my servant, too. She's been here for twelve years, and Lea loves her like a sister. Did you two have a falling out?"

Gods, this was ridiculous, and Mik seriously considered jumping up, and walking out. But his mother reached and grasped his fist on the table, closing it in her cool fingers, and Mik shot her an uneasy look, frowned back at the table.

"She's not happy," he said finally. "With what I'm giving her."

There was an instant's silence, his mother's fingers squeezing on his own. "And you weren't able to reach some kind of compromise?"

Mik shot her another flat, suspicious look. "Like what?"

She looked visibly uncomfortable, suddenly, her eyes glancing brief toward the closed door. "Well," she said, "I suppose I always expected, once you had the means—that you would pension Kay off, and set her up somewhere close by."

Wait. Mik stared at his mother, felt his hand flex under hers. "That I would *keep* her?" he demanded. "Like a permanent *mistress*?"

His mother twitched a helpless, uncomfortable little shrug, and staring at her, it dawned on Mik that this was exactly what she meant. His own mother, suggesting that he keep his housemaid as a *mistress*, and he gaped at her, even as the sudden, mouthwatering idea of it clamped firm in his gut.

"You would actually be *fine* with that?" he demanded at her. "What about Lea? And my future wife?"

His mother gave another of those helpless shrugs, her eyes sliding away from his. "Lea already knows something is going on between you two," she replied. "And not that I condone unfaithfulness, or untruthfulness to one's wedded partner, but—"

"But what?" Mik shot back. "What, Mother?"

She let out a heavy sigh, and frowned down at the table. "It is what men of your station do," she said, "when they marry for duty, rather than affection."

Mik kept staring at her, digesting those words, and the surging beautiful possibility still lingering behind them. His mother knew. She almost *approved*. Despite the fact that Mik's own father had had multiple mistresses hanging off his purse-strings for decades on end, and his mother had known that, and hated it, and Mik had always sworn to do better, to be better. And now this?!

"You really wouldn't judge me?" he heard himself say, his eyes intently studying hers. "Or think less of me? See me as becoming like my father?"

His mother gave a wan little smile, her fingers squeezing tight on his. "I could not think less of you for loving a girl like Kay," she said finally. "And you will always be a better man than your father, Mikkal. No matter what decisions you might make."

Well. Mik's thoughts were racing now, his heartbeat keeping time inside his chest, and he felt something like exhilaration, rising to consume the uneasy unsettled misery in its entirety. He could make Kay his own permanent mistress. Set her up nearby. And she could even keep up her painting hobby, it would be the best of all possible worlds, and why the *hell* hadn't he thought of it sooner.

"But what—what if," he stammered, as the elation plunged again, lingering on that one undeniable snag. "What if there were—children. People would talk. Think less of her. And I wouldn't be able to recognize them. Or be a real father to them."

His mother grimaced, and her hand on Mik's convulsed, just slightly. Thinking, perhaps, of his father's own bastards, multiple half-siblings that Mik had never met, likely some that his father hadn't met, either.

"You'll have to decide if having children out of such a liaison is worth those consequences," she said slowly. "But many men of our station do so, and unlike your father, some do maintain relationships with the children. Personal as well as financial."

Gods curse her, curse him, because again, this was—

permission. Approval. Mik's mother saying she would accept him doing this, siring bastards on his housemaid. And gods, the *thought* of that—his Kay, swelled full with his growing child—was doing thoroughly inappropriate things to Mik's rapidly tightening groin.

"And would *you* accept those children?" he demanded. "If I brought them around here?"

His mother grimaced again, looking down at her hand, still clenching on his. "I would, if you wished," she said carefully. "But your future wife may have another opinion on the matter."

Of course, back to that tedious wife again, but the idea of the rest of it, the possibility, the gods-damned *hopefulness*, had only lodged itself deeper in Mik's thoughts. He could keep Kay. He could prevent her from leaving. He could deal with this, fix this, like a real lord would.

"Thank you, Mother," he said, low and fervent. "Thank you."

And without waiting for her to reply, he leapt to his feet, and rushed off to find Kay.

4

No matter where Mik looked, he could not find Kay.

It was still technically her working hours, so he spent over an hour prowling through the manor, looking through its twenty-odd rooms, where she should have been, by rights, cleaning. But there was no sign of her anywhere, not even in the servants' quarters, or in her little studio upstairs.

And the studio—Mik came to a standstill in the doorway, blinking at it in the sun's fading light through the nearby window—was almost entirely empty. Not crammed full like it usually was, but instead looking forlorn and forgotten, with the shelves for Kay's books and supplies standing vacant, the tall easels bare and bereft of their usual intricate, colourful canvases.

Mik stood in the room for far too long, turning slowly in place, studying what Kay had left behind. Dried palettes and old brushes, likely too worn to be useful. Spattered old drop cloths, which had probably belonged to the manor at some point. And only a few paintings, a few animals and still life studies, and—Mik hesitated, stepped closer—a large canvas Kay had been working on, of them. Him, his mother, Lea.

Kay had asked them to sit for it months ago, shyly claiming that she needed more practice in formal portraiture, and so of course they had obliged her, first posing together for multiple preliminary studies, and then dressing early one day for an evening event. And here they were, his mother and Lea seated, with Mik standing behind, all looking toward the viewer— toward Kay—with kindly, tolerant eyes.

Mik could still remember watching Kay as she'd worked on it, biting her lip, her gaze flicking between them and her canvas, while her brushes had hovered and soared around her. Simultaneously mixing paints, dipping themselves into pots and palettes, and creating her vision on the canvas before her. She'd only occasionally used her hands, perhaps on particularly tricky spots, but she'd still managed to collect a few spatters of paint anyway, some spraying across her cheek, some on the old tunic she'd been wearing. An old tunic of Mik's, in fact.

It had been almost mesmerizing watching her work, and undeniably arousing, and Mik had been deeply grateful for his position at the back of the grouping, where the bulge in his trousers wouldn't be evident to his mother or Lea. But it had been evident to Kay, of course, and afterwards she'd teased him mercilessly about it, threatening to make him pose for her in certain compromising positions.

This painting, at least, was mostly proper, as Mik's crotch was draped in shadow, with only a slight—perhaps normal— bulge visible. But his face—Mik squinted, stepped closer to the painting—was just slightly flushed, his eyes bright. And though he knew he was a decent-looking fellow most days, here he looked almost excessively, impossibly handsome. His jaw sharp, his nose perfectly straight, his mouth firm, his brown waves tumbling slightly over his forehead.

And whether or not it was an overly flattering likeness, it

was most certainly him, undeniably so, and just the same with his mother and Lea. So many artists couldn't quite reach the reality of their subjects—there was so often something off around the eyes, or the mouth—but Kay had captured them thoroughly, completely, almost as though in life. And her words were rising in Mik's head again, *I know you may not see me as a real artist, Mik, but plenty of other people do...*

The unease had begun to twist again in Mik's gut, becoming more of a gnawing, empty ache, and he spun on his heel, and walked out. He needed to find Kay. Needed to talk to her, needed to fix this. He would fix this.

But she was still nowhere to be found, and finally Mik swallowed his pride, and went back to his mother, who was now playing cards in the drawing room with Lea, and asked her where in the gods' green earth Kay could have gone. And it turned out that his mother had decided to give Kay every evening after supper off for the next week, so that she could spend some time at her new place, preparing it for her forthcoming move.

Mik had barely been able to conceal his shocked disbelief—Kay had a new place, already? And after requesting, and failing, to receive sufficient details on the subject from either his mother or Lea—beyond the fact that it was somewhere near Ashon, the closest town—he finally resigned himself to joining them for a few games, during which he twitched and frowned and glared over his shoulder at every creak in the hallway.

By the end of it, even Lea was giving him odd, uncertain glances, and Mik finally claimed exhaustion, and stalked back up to his empty room. Where there was still no Kay, and the only evidence of her ever being there was that damned feather duster, lying so innocuously on the mantel.

He tried first to read, then to practice a new air-spell he'd been working on, and then to review some of the estate paperwork Scullen had left for him. But it was all useless, a complete tedious waste, because Mik's brain had apparently turned to sludge, and finally he just lay there on the bed in the candlelight, staring at nothing.

Had he insulted Kay so badly? If he'd come home, on his usual two-week schedule, would she have carried on, as always? Or had it been what he'd said about her not being an artist? Or maybe how he'd failed her fucked-up test with the pregnancy spell? But, then again, if she had a new place, that meant she'd been planning this for some time, and if he'd stayed away longer, would he have come home to find her *gone*?

The more he thought, the more of a mess it became, and perhaps he did finally doze, late into the evening. Until—his eyes snapped open, his head craning toward the door—there was a quiet click of his door latch, a creak of the hinge. She'd come.

It had to be well after midnight, Mik knew, but that was because Kay would have had to wait until the other servants were asleep to slip out again. And she would still have to wake again before dawn, and Mik fought down the guilt as he slowly sat up on the bed, and looked at her in the dim light of the sputtering candle.

She looked just as tired as he felt, her face shadowed and grim, stark against the white of her simple cotton sleeping shift. But she was here, and beautiful, and all the words vanished in Mik's throat as she slowly padded toward him, without stopping, until she'd climbed up to straddle his sitting form on the bed, and kissed him.

Mik groaned into her mouth, deep and guttural, and willingly let himself be pushed backwards, flat onto the bed. While his own sleeping shirt unbuttoned itself, shoving open wide to reveal his bare chest, and Kay's shift flew off over her head, leaving her pale and naked before him.

And all at once she was here again, warm and desperate

above him, her hands sliding on his bare chest, her mouth kissing hungry and frantic against his. While Mik kissed back hard, just as desperate, his hands dragging her down over him, grabbing and gripping on her shoulders, her back, her arse.

He was already rock-hard, his dick grinding painfully up against her through his trousers, and with a quick thrust of his hand, a kick of his feet, the trousers were off, on the floor. And Kay's hot slick heat was right *there*, sliding against the head of him—and then sinking down, hard, taking him deep inside, while Mik groaned aloud, and she smothered her scream in his shoulder.

Fuck, it was good, and fuck, he'd needed this, and he drove up as she drove down, meeting with pain and power and pleasure. Harsh and unrelenting and glorious, her teeth on his lips, his hands yanking her hair, her body quivering and craving around him, full of his dick, soon to be full of his seed. And he didn't give a damn, he didn't, and fuck, he had to *say*—

"Want to come in you," he gasped. "Make you *mine*, Kay."

Her weight on him went oddly, suddenly still, though her tight heat around him was frantically, rhythmically clenching, betraying her body's undeniable pleasure for him, for those words. But her eyes on his face were shocked and staring, her peaked breasts heaving over him with the harsh gasps of her breath.

"What?" she said, her voice blank, scraping. "But the—the *pregnancy spell*, Mik."

"Don't care," he breathed. "If it's what you want."

The shock shivered again through Kay's form, stuttering across her face, and perhaps to prove his point, Mik ground his hips up, hard. Bringing back the heat, the hunger, he was fucking his best girl, he would fill her with his seed, she would grow his babes and bear his children, always his, marked and owned, *forever*—

"*No*," Kay said, almost a wail, like a pail of cold water on

Mik's face—and he blinked at her, fought to keep up, as she yanked her still-heaving body up and off him, leaving his dick wet, wilting, bereft. And him perhaps just the same, his mouth very near to begging or perhaps sobbing, and she stared at him, her hands fluttering against her lips, she was saying no, *no*.

But then in a stilted, shaky movement, she shoved herself down between Mik's legs, thrusting them apart, kneeling low over him—and then she sucked his half-hard dick deep into her hungry, wet mouth. While her hands stroked and grasped and caressed around it, finding his balls his hips his taint, as she slurped and moaned around his rapidly hardening length.

Mik was barely keeping up at this point, could only watch and feel and revel in it, his Kay lavishing him as though her life depended on it. Taking his full length deep into her convulsing throat, without even a twitch of hesitation this time, while her lips sucked hard around the base of him, her face buried in the thick coarse hair of his groin. While her hands kept frantically sliding and grasping on his balls, between his sprawled legs, one long finger already finding his tight puckered heat—and then slowly delving inside, *fuck*, while Mik bucked and hissed and moaned.

It was pleasure unlike anything else, unlike anything any other girl had ever done, pulling him apart piece by piece. That long finger curving and caressing deep inside, his prick deep in her gagging throat, her hand clutching at his tightening balls so hard it hurt—and her eyes, her eyes on his were like one at worship, at prayer, at complete and utter supplication to her lord, pleading for his sweet, rich bounty.

Mik came with a shout, perhaps almost a scream, as his raging prick finally, *finally* capitulated, and exploded his pleasure. Surging his seed hot and thick into his supplicant's eager mouth in pulse after pulse, each one a blaring stream of impossible pleasure, made even more impossible by the rhythmic swallows of her throat around it, the deep vibrations of her own desperate groans, the adoration of her bright grey eyes on his.

She didn't let off until Mik was entirely empty, his whole body trembling with the aftershocks, shaky and sweaty and wrung out. Still blinking at her with dazed, hazy eyes as her finger drew out, her hand on his balls eased up, and her swollen pink mouth finally pulled off his limp, sated prick. Still doing it slow, worshipful even now, baptizing him in the gentle slide of her mouth. In the soft, sweet kiss at the end, her tongue slipping inside his skin to whisper to his open, sensitive slit before finally, finally pulling away for good.

Mik was still staring at her, still entirely and wholly lost, and he watched his shaky hand come up, stroke slow and wondering down her red cheek. "You don't want my baby, love?" he whispered, his voice hoarse, choked. "And are you— are you saying *goodbye* to me?"

Kay's mouth convulsed, her eyes far too bright—and then those eyes spilled over, and she was sobbing. Sitting between Mik's spread legs and openly weeping, the tears streaking down her face, the shuddering breaths gasping from her throat.

Something twisted in Mik's chest, almost hard enough to break—and in a sudden, lurching movement he was sitting up too, and dragging her trembling body into his arms. Feeling her shudder and sob and gasp against him, her tears dripping onto his bare shoulder, and he could feel the water welling in his own eyes too, why, what the fuck had he done.

He stayed there in silence, his arms as tight around her as they would go, until her sobs had finally faded, faltering into broken, hiccoughing gasps. "Gods," she said, "I'm sorry, Mik, I know me bawling in your bed is the last thing you want to deal with, I just—"

But Mik shook his head, pulling back enough to press his fingers against her lips. "Hey," he said, his voice soft, despite the guilt she'd just wrenched into his chest. "Of course I want you here, however you're feeling, I just—I don't *understand*, Kay."

Kay's breath had begun hitching again, veering back toward the sobs, and Mik pulled in a breath, and made himself say what should have been said, years ago. "I don't want to lose you," he whispered. "I can't stand the idea of losing you, Kay. And if you'll let me, I'll fix this for both of us. I'll get you a place of your own, some money to live on, as many painting supplies as you want. And we can still do this, whenever you like. And if it's kids you want, I'll support you, and do whatever I can for them. All right?"

He watched her eyes as he spoke, searching for her response, but he couldn't quite seem to read it, or follow that odd tilt to her breath. "All right?" he asked. "Say yes, Kay. It'll fix everything."

But Kay wasn't saying yes, Kay was staring at the wall behind him, her eyes blinking back what looked to be fresh tears. Still upset, after being handed an offer like that, and Mik truly wasn't following now, not the sudden stiffness in her form, or the tightness spreading on her mouth.

"It won't fix everything, Mik," she replied, the words sinking like stones into his gut. "It might fix everything for you, but it fixes *nothing* for me. It'll just mean that I'm trapped at your whim even more, just living on your handouts, stuck there waiting for whenever you decide to come home, while also raising your children *alone!*"

Good gods, that was not at all what he'd meant, and Mik opened his mouth to tell her so—but now Kay put her fingers to his lips, pressing tight. "No," she said, her voice cracking. "You're still not listening, Mik. I said, I want my own life. I want my own work. I want my own family. And taking your money to be constantly available to you—even if it means I get to have your children—is still *none* of that. Because we both know your real family will be here, with a woman who isn't me!"

Fuck, she was still on that, and Mik moved her hand from his mouth, perhaps rougher than he meant. "You *are* my real family, Kay," he countered. "You always have been, and that will never change. No matter who else is in the picture."

But Kay only laughed, the sound strange, high-pitched. "And you think that's good?" she demanded. "If *I'm* your real family, Mik, then that poor woman you're marrying, and those poor children she'll give you, are *not*. And even the most tolerant woman in the world isn't going to stand for you having your real family elsewhere, and parading that fact under her nose!"

Mik's anger was beginning to rise, now, and with it a pointed hurt, curdling under his skin. "Oh, bullshit," he snapped back. "People of my station do it all the time, and my wife will accept it, if I tell her to. Look at my parents, they lived completely separate lives, and my mother dealt with it just fine!"

But Kay was staring at Mik like he'd grown two heads, and she shoved herself away from him, out of his arms entirely. "Dear gods, Mik," she said, "do you honestly think that what your father did to your family was *fine*? And do you really think your mother was happy, raising you two here all alone, while her husband fucked around the capital, spent all her hard work on gaming and harlots, and only came home long enough to slap her around, and make his kids feel like shit?"

Mik blinked at her, and suddenly he felt deeply affronted, and thoroughly, irrationally furious. "I am *not* my father," he breathed. "I would never do what my father did. I would never hurt the people I loved like that."

But the laugh from Kay's mouth was hard, bitter, miserable. "Don't look now, *my lord*," she said, "but you already have."

Mik felt completely lost, again, and Kay rose unsteadily to her feet, and turned to face him, her shoulders heaving. "I've loved you for ten years, Mik," she hissed. "And you *wanted* me to love you. You touched me, teased me, made me laugh, made me your own. You turned me into exactly what you want in bed, and then you kept me here, for years, so you could have me whenever you wanted. You told me you cared for me, you gave me gifts, you praised me, called me your best girl. But in truth"—she dragged in a thick, choked breath—"I'm your *possession*, Mik. And you don't write to your possessions, you don't tell them when you're coming home, you don't have a real family with them. They're *disposable*, Mik."

Mik desperately fought to sort through that, to find the lies in those words, but maybe they weren't lies, maybe they were something else. "But you wanted it, Kay," he said, pleaded, and that was true, it was. "You know it wasn't all me. You made me into what you like too, you *like* being with me, playing these games with me. And we're friends, we're best friends, we've grown up together, we both know each other better than anyone else in the world. You're the opposite of disposable. You're—you're *everything*, Kay. I love you more than anyone else *alive*."

Kay's eyes snapped wide, her hand scrubbing at her mouth, but she still took a step backwards, gave a slow, measured shake of her head. "If that was really true," she said, her voice unsteady, "you would have found another way, Mik. You would offer to make me a partner, and not a plaything."

And with those impossible words ringing in the air, she snapped her sleeping shift on over her head, and left.

5

Mik slept badly that night, tossing and turning in hot sticky sheets, and starting awake again and again. From dreams of Kay, snippets of awful words like *possession* and *disposable*. And when he finally saw the light easing through the window, he fervently thanked the gods, and all but hurled himself out of bed.

He had to return to Coven Manor that evening—he was directing a seminar first thing the next morning—which meant that he had a mountain of estate work to burn through before he left. So he fought to think about that list of tasks, and not about Kay, as he rapidly dressed, and strode outside in the direction of Smit's farm.

But his thoughts kept winding toward Kay anyway, especially since he would usually have brought her along with him to help handle this. And once he arrived at the farm, Smit clearly thought as much too, and kept looking around behind Mik's back, as if Kay were liable to pop up at any moment.

"How many fields do you need done?" Mik asked, voice clipped. "And how much water?"

Smit demonstrated with a width of fingers, and Mik

nodded, and followed him toward the nearest grain field—but Smit kept looking around, peering down the path behind them. "When's that girl of yours showing up?" he said. "One who keeps us dry? I don't have a clean change of clothes, mind you."

Mik bit back a groan, and gave a hard wave of his hand toward the sky above them, pushing up the warm air, dragging the cool air down. "She's not coming."

"But now we'll get all wet," Smit protested, and it was true, because making it rain—and as much rain as Smit wanted— was not an easy task, and not one that would allow Mik to maintain air-shields over their heads at the same time. Which was, ostensibly, why Mik had always brought Kay, because she had a clever little spell that could keep textiles dry—not to mention the fact that she was also an excellent hand at dealing with people like Smit, and therefore made the entire proceedings far less painful for all involved.

"Then go stand under something," Mik snapped, which Smit did, trotting away without another word. Leaving Mik to drag and weave the darkening clouds above them, pushing and pulling the magic again and again, until there was a huge, swirling storm crackling above them, rising rising rising—and then the clouds opened up, and rain hammered down.

Usually hurling out rainstorms was a deeply satisfying experience, one that was made even better with Kay keeping him warm and dry, and staring wide-eyed and pink-cheeked at the clouds above. Even though she'd seen him do it hundreds of times, now, she'd never seemed to lose her awe of it, and had looked at Mik as though he were a marvel, or a god.

But there was no one watching him now, not even Smit, and Mik was already soaked to the skin and shivering. And he didn't even wait for Smit to follow along before stalking over to the next field, and doing it again, and again, and again.

The morning passed with tedious slowness, field after field, storm after storm. And when it was finally done, it was near midday, and Mik felt numb all over, and nearly too exhausted to stand.

But that didn't mean relief was in sight, quite the opposite, because he needed to see Scullen, too. And even a quick cup of soup from the manor's kitchen and a change into warm clothes couldn't seem to take the cold off, or the hollow misery that just kept rising with every endless hour. *Your possession*, she'd said. *Disposable.*

"So what's the most pressing?" he said to Scullen, once Scullen was in his study, sitting opposite his desk. "I don't have much time."

Scullen was the estate's man of business, a position he'd held for the past few years, once Mik's father had gone too far to care, and his mother had appointed a man to her own liking instead. And while Mik trusted Scullen, he didn't always like him, and part of the reason was this, the way the cranky old coot blinked balefully at Mik over the half-moon glasses perched on his hooked nose.

"It is all pressing, your lordship," he said, in his slow, deliberate monotone. "You have bonds in dire need of re-investment, priorities to decide upon regarding tenant repairs, and a rapidly growing sinkhole near Jenkens' farm. Also, Benk's wife is ill, and requires treatment beyond what he can afford, and half your fields are drying up—though I note you did deign to visit Smit's this morning, very well—and there has been another significant debt come to light, claimed against your mortgage."

Mik couldn't help an exasperated groan—that last bit would be his father, still sending his well-wishes a year beyond the grave—and he sighed, rubbed his hands against his mouth. "And were you able to find the coin I asked for?"

That had been a late request, one Mik had sent in just this morning, and Scullen gave him another reproachful look as he reached into his satchel, pulled out a clinking bag, and dropped it onto the desk between them. "Given the current state of your affairs, your lordship," he said, "I cannot help but point out that drawing such generous amounts from your limited liquid assets is ill-advised."

Mik groaned again, and resisted the irrational urge to kick over the desk, and stalk out of the room altogether. "Fine, fine, let's start at the beginning," he snapped, with a last grasp at his patience. "What do you need?"

Thus commenced three hours of laborious, difficult discussion, during which Mik was required to make rapid, often unsatisfactory decisions on subjects he often knew very little about. Subjects that had true repercussions on other people's actual lives and happiness, and for which he, solely, stood responsible.

It was part of why he so desperately needed a wife—he was a mage, not a secretary, and he'd never possessed the patience, or the mental organization, to keep track of multiple other people's situations and personalities and ongoing needs. Though he had to admit, as Scullen reproachfully and thoroughly explained several points that Mik likely should have known, that if he were just *here* more often, this would all be a hell of a lot easier.

He finally left his study feeling bone-weary and grim, with the bag of coins clutched in his fingers. He only had a few hours of daylight left, he had to get on the road to Coven Manor—but first, he had to find Kay.

He didn't waste his energy wandering this time, and instead went straight to his mother, who was reading in the sunroom. "Where's Kay?" he asked, without preamble. "I have to leave soon."

"Yes, of course," his mother said, her voice smooth, and gods, that was a twinge of reproach in her eyes, too. "Last I saw, she was cleaning in the great room."

Her eyebrows were raised expectantly, her eyes darting a pointed glance at the bag in Mik's hand, asking him the silent question. And in reply he gave the silent answer, a hard shake of his head, before turning on his heel, and stalking for the great room.

Kay was indeed there, cleaning, with her back to the door. Her feather duster was alternately sliding and swooping, making her typical little loops again, while behind her a broom neatly and efficiently swept a small pile of dirt across the floor. All without even the slightest movement of Kay's hands, and Mik leaned against the door frame to watch, while a tight lump formed in his throat.

She really was brilliant. Graceful, talented, clever, his own poised, regal, brush-wielding goddess. Except that she wasn't, anymore, and this might be the last time he ever watched her do this, and the lump in Mik's throat swelled even larger, until it seemed to swallow his breath. This was it. She was leaving.

He had to clear his throat, find air again, and at the sound Kay whirled around, both the brush and the broom clattering to the floor at once. And now she was looking at him, not moving or speaking, and Mik dragged up his courage, and made himself walk across the room toward her.

"My apologies for interrupting," he heard himself say, far too formal. "But I need to return to Coven Manor tonight, and wished to speak to you first."

Kay twitched a little nod, her unusually shadowed eyes not quite meeting his, and Mik pulled in another heavy, shaky breath. "I apologize if I have hurt you, or treated you unfairly," he said. "I am so thankful for you, and the years you have spent in our service. I wish you nothing but the best, Kay, and hope that you'll accept this"—he held the small bag out toward her—"as a token of my gratitude."

Kay blinked at him, and then at the bag, eyeing it as though it were something dangerous—but then she reached a careful, trembly hand, and took it from Mik's fingers. And then, with a flicker of magic, she slid the top of the bag open, revealing the glittering contents inside.

"*Mik*," she gasped, and her eyes on his were shocked, aghast. "This—this must be twice what I make in a *year*."

Mik shrugged, and his mouth twisted. "I didn't realize I'd been underpaying you so badly," he replied, his voice still too formal. "In which case, it's still not even close to what I fully owe you."

Kay blinked between him, and the bag, and the look on her face was helpless, perhaps even pleading. "*Mik*," she said again, "that wasn't you, it was your father, you can't afford this."

Mik tried to shrug again, to force his face into some semblance of a smile. "You deserve it," he told her. "And this way you'll have some time to build your business the way you really want to. Until you become a household name, and people are falling all over themselves to buy a beautiful painting from the brilliant Kay Courser."

Kay's mouth opened and closed, clearly readying an argument, but before she could get started, Mik raised a hand, and shot a quelling puff of warm air toward her. "And *please* don't argue," he added. "I'll have to insist, or else hide it in your belongings when you're not looking, and then we'll part on even worse terms than we already are."

He attempted another smile, but miserably failed, because suddenly that lump was in his throat again, stealing away his breath. And Kay didn't smile back, didn't even look at him, just kept blinking at that bag in her now-clenched hand.

"Listen, Mik," she said, her voice hitching. "I know what I said to you last night, and I still mean it. But"—she briefly glanced up, grey eyes too bright—"you've been family to me too. You've been a true friend. You've been generous and supportive of me and so very kind. I will"—she drew in a slow, shaky breath—"I'll never forget you, or all you've done for me."

But it was goodbye. It was his Kay sending him away, not just now, but forever. And gods, Mik felt like he was going to be sick, felt like the room was spinning around him, and there was no footing, no purchase left. Except, maybe, maybe—

"Perhaps," he made himself say, "perhaps you'll let me write you? Once you're settled?"

Kay's eyes darted up again, and there was something in them he couldn't at all read. "Perhaps," she said, but there were no words beyond that, no explanation, no suggestion of her new coordinates. No hint that she would even welcome that, now that Mik had so thoroughly fucked this up, without even realizing what he'd done.

"Right," he said, through that still-rising lump in his throat, now desperately threatening to escape. "Very well. Best wishes, Kay."

And with that, he turned and walked away, before she could see the tears filling his eyes, and finally spilling down his face.

6

M ik arrived back at the Coven Manor for Magical Advancement late, well after dark.

It had felt like an endless ride, despite being one he'd made hundreds of times before, and the further he went from home, the more it felt like he was making an irreparable, fatal mistake. Like he'd horribly miscalculated an important answer, somehow, without even knowing what the question had been.

At least being back at Coven Manor would help, he told himself, as he and his horse Leni approached its open, well-kept grounds, and the warden cheerfully opened the iron gate to admit them. Coven Manor had been Mik's home away from home for the past five years, and had provided him with money and purpose when he'd desperately needed it. And while it had various politics and issues of its own, still it remained the top magical facility in the country, with forty-odd expert young mages working and training on-site, and many more rotating in and out as needed.

Mik was currently one of the top-ranking air-mages at Coven Manor, often called upon to lead projects and training, and he'd found that his own unconventional education—more through tutors and short sessions, rather than the usual years-long stints at the capital's costly academies—had actually worked in his favour, giving him a more practical, multidisciplinary understanding of air-magic than most. He was well-respected at Coven Manor, and well-liked, and once he'd stabled Leni and stepped into the manor's familiar stone entry hall, he could almost believe that everything was normal. Everything was fine.

That was, until he'd rounded the corner toward the staircase, and nearly plowed head-on into one of Coven Manor's servants, who was carrying a full armful of clean folded linens. And of course, the linens went flying, the servant went skidding, and when Mik reached out to grab her, hurling a protective air-shield beneath her blonde head at the same time, he realized, too late, that it was Annie.

And that meant he was holding Annie in his arms, her blue eyes blinking up at him in the wall sconce's flickering light, and her face was flushed, her slim chest heaving under her maid's uniform. And her mouth slowly curved upwards, her eyebrow lifting with a clear suggestion, and Mik briefly squeezed his eyes shut as he rapidly disentangled himself, and set her on her feet, a safe distance away.

"Sorry," he said. "You all right?"

Annie's head was tilting, clearly considering that question for all it was worth, and Mik silently cursed himself, and particularly his past self, of five years previously. Because when he'd first come to Coven Manor, and Annie had made her availability to him extensively clear, Mik had looked at her blonde hair, her slim supple body, her maid's uniform—and he'd thought of Kay, and agreed.

And while it had become swiftly, abundantly clear that fucking a girl like Annie was an entirely different and far more complicated matter than fucking Kay had been, Mik had kept at it for far longer than any decent fellow should have. Only finally putting a stop to it when he realized that Annie was not Kay, would never be Kay, and also, that Annie had been fucking at least three of his fellow mages at the same time.

"I'm not certain I *am* well, my lord," Annie said, in a voice that was entirely too innocent. "Perhaps you could help me back to the servants' quarters? With a little stop by your room, if you like?"

Mik's room was on the fourth floor, on the entirely opposite end of the Manor from the servants' quarters, and he couldn't quite bite back his unsympathetic snort. "Sorry, I'm busy," he replied. "But I can go fetch Oden or Ela to help, if you need."

Oden and Ela were the head housekeepers, and Annie clearly wasn't interested in their assistance, judging by the wrinkle of distaste on her pert nose. "Are you certain, my lord?" she asked. "It's been so long, and I'd be honoured to repay you for your chivalry. You'll be pleased, I'm sure."

She accompanied the words with a wink, and a casual, surreptitious slip of her hand into her dress pocket. A movement that had perhaps been entirely unconscious, but Mik's eyes suddenly caught on it, trapped in the implication of it. Because when they'd been doing that, afterwards, Annie had sometimes asked for coin. And Mik had wanted to help, had wanted to be kind to a girl he was fucking, so he'd usually given it.

But perhaps he'd never quite made the connection before—perhaps he hadn't *wanted* to make that connection before—and he felt his face flushing, his stomach clenching with a sharp, curdling nausea.

"Sorry, but no," he said. "Not now, or *ever* again, Annie."

An undeniable hurt flashed across Annie's face, but Mik suddenly couldn't bear to look at her, and turned and stalked away. Leaving her with a mess of linens to clean up, and he briefly thought of Kay again—a single look from her and it would be a neat pile again—and what the *fuck* would Kay say if she knew he'd done that with a girl like Annie.

Mik scrubbed at his eyes as he climbed the thankfully empty stairs to his room, and slammed the door shut with a hard gust of air. His room here was his own private space, had been for years, and the sight of its warm woods and familiar furnishings should have been welcome, comforting—but he still felt oddly, thoroughly shaken, and he sank stiffly down to sit on his bed.

Annie had fucked him for the money. Not because she'd liked him, or maybe even wanted him. She'd fucked him because he was a strong air-mage, and a noble, and therefore, supposedly had money.

Very few people here knew about his family's actual financial situation—Mik had worked very hard to keep that truth under wraps—but if Annie had known the truth, or if he hadn't usually had those small amounts of coin on hand when she'd asked, would she have even looked at him twice? And if she'd truly needed the money badly enough, had propositioning him even been a freely made choice, on her part? Or a necessity?

And, even more appallingly, had it been a freely made choice for *Kay*?

But yes, yes, Mik knew it had been, because when it had started between them, he'd been essentially just as poor as she'd been, just as trapped. And they'd found refuge in each other, hiding from the rest of the servants in broom closets and spare rooms, and it hadn't been until Mik had turned nineteen, and finally accessed some of his grandfather's trusts, that he'd had any money to give.

And even then, it had never been money—Mik's past self had at least recognized that as a bad plan—but gifts. Art supplies and art classes and art books, anything creative that caught Kay's eye. And with those gifts, Kay had turned around and made Mik gifts in return, on a pleasingly regular basis.

Gifts that had even followed him here, and Mik lurched to his feet, lit his candle, and began to silently study them, one by one.

There were multiple framed paintings, several on each wall, ranging from very early—with the requisite now-visible errors—to Kay's more recent, more refined work. They were all realistic depictions of things from Mik's life—his horses, his lands, Lea—and the biggest and most spectacular piece of all was a landscape, an impressively accurate view from the highest point on Mik's lands, looking over Sunem's farm, with a whirl of storm clouds gathering to the east. Where storm clouds didn't usually gather, and that meant it was Mik's storm, immortalized forever with canvas and paint.

There were sketches, too, not framed, but stashed haphazardly about the room. More drawings of home, of his tenants' farms, of the muddy, busy streets of Ashon. There was a lovely one of Lea laughing, perfectly captured with only a few deceptively simple-looking black strokes. And—Mik hesitated, frowning—another likeness of him, looking at the viewer, at Kay. This time with a raised eyebrow, a teasing quirk on his mouth, and it was again brilliantly flattering, making him look almost like a satyr, or a trickster prince from the old fairy tales.

At the time, Mik had welcomed that drawing as appreciatively as he had all the rest, though he could still remember teasing Kay that she'd desperately needed to have her eyes checked. But now, looking at it was doing unsettling things to his gut, because this—*this*—was how Kay had seen him. For ten years. And in return he'd hurt her, and made her feel *disposable*, and fucked another poor housemaid in exchange for coin, just because she'd looked a little like Kay, and—

"Mikkal!" came a voice, from beyond the door. "Are you in there?"

Mik stifled an involuntary groan, but clearly not well enough, because the voice spoke again, unintelligibly this time, as the door clicked open. And here, of course, was Ilsa. Dark-haired and buxom and gorgeous, and dressed only in a see-through sleeping shift. *Damn* Mik's life to hell and back again.

"You *are* here!" Ilsa said, with rather surprising delight, but that was because—Mik stifled another groan—he'd forgotten to actually break it off with her, before he'd left. He'd honestly just had enough, and had mentally called it in, and decided to go see Kay—but he hadn't actually told Ilsa that, or even that he was going to be away. And gods, had he always been this much of a bastard?

"Yeah," he said, rubbing his eyes hard, as he sat back down on the bed. "Sorry, had to go home for a few days. Estate issues to deal with."

And he was being a bastard, again, because that hadn't actually been the reason he'd gone, and in reply Ilsa sashayed over, and put a knee to the bed beside him. "Oh really?" she asked. "Nothing serious, I hope?"

Her voice was light, just a preamble to what she was expecting next—but looking at her, suddenly, it was like a strange, irrational, inexplicable madness had taken over Mik's body, and filled his mouth with words he hadn't at all intended.

"Pretty serious, actually," he heard himself say. "Looks like I might end up losing the whole place."

He'd expected the words to have some effect, but he hadn't quite expected Ilsa to startle like she did, or leap off the bed as though it were suddenly made of swamp muck. "What?" she demanded, high-pitched. "Just the house? Or your whole *estate*?"

Mik's jaw tightened, but he looked up at her with steady eyes. "The whole thing," he said flatly. "Lost to the banks, in payment for my late father's debts."

"*What*?" Ilsa said again, her usual come-hither brown eyes replaced by bulging, white-rimmed discs. "All *eighteen* farms? And all your income? *Forever*?"

Ilsa had never once stepped foot on Mik's estate, and while Mik had probably mentioned, at some point or another, that he had eighteen farms, it was wholly disheartening to realize that Ilsa clearly remembered that fact, when just the week before she'd forgotten Lea's name. And there was still time for Mik to back down from this, he *should* back down from this—but for reasons he couldn't at all explain, he suddenly, desperately needed to know where it led.

"Yes, all gone," Mik said, as smoothly as he could. "And my title along with it, But I'll keep working here, so I'll have some income to live on, at least. Though I'll have to support my mother and Lea with it now, too."

Ilsa was still blinking at him, and gave her head a hard, furious shake. "So you're *impoverished*, and a *commoner*?" she demanded. "Truly, Mikkal?"

"Yep," Mik replied, clipped, and then he sat there in silence, and watched the emotions play across Ilsa's lovely face. Disbelief first, and then horror, as the truth sank in. And then an uneasy discomfort, because—the grim certainty swelled in Mik's gut as he watched—because Ilsa was going to break up with him over this. And she didn't quite know how.

He could see her trying to work it out—whether it was better to do it now, or later, when it wouldn't seem directly tied to his disclosure of his financial troubles. And after giving a quick, furtive glance up and down his seated form, Ilsa seemed to decide it, and came a slow step closer. About to offer him a pity fuck, make it seem like she still cared, and then probably dump him tomorrow or next week. And while maybe Mik should have been flattered that he was still worth a pity fuck, even without the money—suddenly he just felt ill, and cold, and dirty all over.

"Also, Ilsa," he said, voice hard, "I've been meaning to tell you—I want to break it off."

Ilsa blinked again, though he didn't miss the brief flicker of relief across her eyes, tinged with something perhaps like suspicion. "You do?" she asked. "Why?"

Mik took a breath, and looked at her, and considered it. Ilsa was smart and sultry and voluptuous, she'd tried to please him in bed, she'd managed to keep his attention for two whole months. She'd also been friendly and obliging and fun, all the things a guy could want in a girl. And yet, she'd forgotten Lea's name, she'd never once asked about the paintings scattered throughout his room, she'd still been a deathly boring fuck compared to Kay, and also, she was fucking him for the fucking *money*.

"I," Mik began, and then swallowed, raised his chin, and just said it. "There's another girl. Back home."

The shock flared again across Ilsa's face, followed by a slow, creeping disbelief. "Oh, really?" she asked, her voice cool. "And who is she?"

Mik considered that too, turning over the possible answers in his head, until he found the one that felt most like truth. "She's an earth-mage," he said. "And an artist. She's really, really brilliant."

Perhaps more truth rang through in the words than Mik should have let on, because Ilsa was looking distinctly ruffled, perhaps even insulted. "Well, she can't be *that* brilliant, can she?" she asked archly. "If she's not working here?"

Ilsa's meaning, of course, was that she was more brilliant than Kay, because she'd had an expensive education, which had then granted her entrance to the prestigious Coven Manor. And that all came down to money too, and money didn't make you a better mage, or a fucking better *person*, and Mik felt his lip curl, his hands tightening to fists against his blanket.

"She painted *that*," he said firmly, giving a sharp nod toward the painting of Sunem's farm with his swirling rain clouds, almost vivid enough to be real. "So yeah. She's fucking *brilliant*."

There was an instant's shocked silence from Ilsa, staring narrow-eyed at the painting, and then back toward Mik. "Then fuck you too, arsehole," she hissed. "I hope you enjoy your new life as a *pauper*."

With that, she turned and stalked out with as much dignity as she could muster, while wearing a flimsy sleeping shift. Leaving Mik to stare after her, trying to decide whether he should feel guilty, or furious, or just deeply, excessively relieved.

And suddenly he was just too tired to care, and he fell back on the bed, staring at the ceiling. Kay hadn't cared about the money. She'd cared about *him*. She'd spent time with him, she'd made him gifts she'd known he would like, she'd cared about his family, she'd made him laugh, made him beg and gasp and scream.

And what had Mik done, in return? He'd made her his *possession*, she'd said. He'd turned her into exactly what he wanted in bed, and then he'd kept her there, for years, underpaid and lonely, waiting for him to come home.

And it was all true. Wasn't it? He'd wanted Kay there, waiting. He'd wanted to keep her for his own. And half that time—these past five years—he'd been fucking girls like Annie, and Ilsa, and so many others he couldn't even remember their faces. Looking for pleasure, for distraction, for the perfect girl who could finally replace Kay.

But maybe there was no replacement for Kay, after all. And in trying to replace her, Mik had finally lost her, for good.

7

I f Mik had expected Ilsa to keep quiet about their breakup, the next morning proved him disastrously wrong.

It began the instant he stepped out of his bedroom, with a few side-eyed glances and whispers from the other mages passing by. His colleagues, in fact, Njall and Tomik, who didn't so much as say good morning, but kept right on walking, with a murmur of furtive discomfort trailing behind them.

Mik briefly considered using an air-spell to eavesdrop on what was being said, but after another similar encounter on the next floor down, it became irrevocably clear what the fuss was about. Not so much about him and Ilsa—nasty breakups were regular rumour fodder in a place like this—but about his estate, and his title. Or the so-called lack thereof.

And clearly, Mik hadn't quite realized the extent to which his lands and his title had affected the way the people around him regarded him. Because in addition to the looks and the whispers, there were even a few jeers and snickers—not from people Mik cared about, or had ever been close to, but still, it stung more than he would have liked to admit.

His seminar that morning, which should have been a straightforward review of key weather spells for some less-weather-inclined air-mages, was a particularly sobering experience. All five of the mages were younger, and newer to Coven Manor, all of them wealthy, and several with lands and titles themselves. And suddenly, it seemed that learning magic from an old, disgraced has-been was an affront, and their response to Mik's demonstrations varied from sidelong glances to outright dissension.

"Are you sure that's how hot the air has to be?" countered one of them, a scrawny guy named Kass, who happened to also be the eldest son of the Earl of Levis, and who had recently, Mik clearly remembered, tried to proposition Lea at a dinner party. "That's not what they taught at the Academy."

"Well, then they're wrong," Mik replied flatly. "Because this is how it's done. Unless you want your storm to fall in on itself in two minutes."

Kass eyed Mik with open disbelief, and leaned over to elbow at his friend. "He didn't even go to the Air Academy," he said, in a whisper that was fully audible to all the surrounding mages. "How's he supposed to know?"

Mik was rapidly losing his temper with everything and everyone, and stalked over to Kass, leaning far too close. "Then why don't you show us," he snapped. "Right here, right now. What's a proper Academy storm look like."

It was a sorry way to teach, putting someone on the spot like that with all his buddies watching, but apparently Mik was just a sorry human being, because he waved the clouds over with a hard flick of his hand. "I'll even get it started for you," he said. "Now prove me wrong."

Thus began a deeply unpleasant two hours, during which Mik was grimly and thoroughly proven correct, and in the process made permanent enemies of all five of his students. Several of whom made no secret of their intent to inform their department's director, Klaus Ketill, of Mik's so-called aggression and unprofessionalism, and thereby landed Mik with a summons to Ketill's office, several hours later.

"Lord Ryning," Ketill said, looking over his spectacles toward Mik across his desk, and Mik was sharply, oppressively reminded of Scullen, just the day before. "Or should I say, Mr. Mastersson?"

Mik was thoroughly enraged by this point, and barely kept himself in his seat. "Call me whatever you like, Mr. Ketill," he replied, voice clipped. "What's your reason for asking me here?"

"I have been informed," Ketill said, with maddening steadiness, "that your seminar this morning was below our esteemed facility's usual standards."

Mik pinched the bridge of his nose, and looked back at Ketill's face. "I admit to being harsher than usual," he replied. "But I would also presume, Mr. Ketill, that our esteemed facility's 'usual standards' would also apply to extending basic courtesy to one's far more experienced instructor!"

Ketill only gazed blandly back toward him, his fingers drumming on the desk. "You are aware, I am sure," he said, "that the Earl of Levis is a member of the Coven's upper Council, as well as one of this facility's principal funders."

Mik leaned forward in his chair, resting his elbows on Ketill's glossy wooden desk. "With all due respect, Mr. Ketill, no matter how much money the Earl of Levis gives, or wherever he stands in the Coven, his son has *no right* to be here. His control is terrible, his power is terrible, he couldn't even make a basic rainstorm. I've seen better air-magic from eight-year-olds."

Ketill just kept looking at him, blinking over those spectacles, and too late the comprehension flooded Mik's thoughts, all at once. Ketill knew that Kass was a terrible air-mage, and he didn't *care*.

"I have been instructed to file a complaint with the Council regarding your conduct," Ketill finally said, leaning back in his chair. "I will do so, with the caveat that you have reportedly experienced some recent personal and financial—*difficulties*—that may have affected your performance."

What? Ketill might as well have hurled a blast of snow in Mik's face, and Mik was two seconds away from retorting that his only difficulties were related to Ilsa's big fat mouth, which had repeatedly proven itself incapable of even taking a proper dick down its throat—and gods, Mik was losing it, was losing his fucking mind. *Had* he taught useless mages here before? He had, perhaps, but he had never pushed them like that, demanded to see what they were really capable of. And clearly he should have, because was Coven Manor infested with useless mages? Was *he* a useless mage? What the hell was happening to him?

"If that's all, then," he mumbled, shoving to his feet, "I'd like to be excused."

But there was suddenly a slight presence in the air behind him—a wall, Ketill was blocking him in with a *wall*—and Ketill leaned forward on his desk, steepling his fingers together. "Before you depart, Mr. Mastersson," he said calmly, "let me be perfectly clear. Our facility does have certain standards, which our mages are required to uphold. And if you prove yourself unwilling or incapable of meeting those standards, you will face the decreed consequences."

It was total and utter bollocks, and Mik glared down at Ketill, with an entirely new contempt for the man ringing through his entire being. "And what are those consequences?" he demanded. "You'll fire me?"

Ketill's prim, pursed mouth said as much, and Mik shoved the chair back, and shoved through Ketill's dissolving shield. "Like hell," he said. "You try it, and I'll quit first."

And with that, he stalked out of the room, and slammed the door shut behind him.

8

Mik spent the rest of the day hovering somewhere between a towering rage, and a fit of full-on despair. Complete with a generous measure of thorough, surprisingly bitter contempt toward his own massively ignorant self of only three days past.

How had he not noticed? How had he not realized what the world around him truly looked like? His position here was a sham, his magic might very well be a sham, his prowess with women was without question a humiliating, appalling fucking sham.

And Kay. Kay had been the truth to the sham, she'd liked his magic, she'd liked *him*, she'd shown it with words and actions and ropes, and what had Mik done? Made her into a possession. Made her *disposable*.

And if Kay was here, if it was like before, she would probably have dismissed all of Coven Manor away, with a single disdainful glance of her grey eyes. *Of course they're full of rubbish*, she might have said. *What else did you expect? Now, as for* you, *my lord...*

At that point she'd have been backing him up, maybe into a

wall or his own air-shield, with her hand on his chest, or his mouth, or his dick. And she'd be gauging him, perhaps, weighing how to play it, and once she saw how truly upset he was, she'd have held it out as an offer. His choice.

I think your lordship needs to be taught a few hard lessons, she might say, with a smug smile, snapping that feather duster into her hand. *Unless you think you can stop me.*

And it would have been permission. A gift. Allowing Mik to lose his shit here, with her, where it was safe. Either taking it out on her, barking orders and pushing her around, holding her down as he drove his dick into her throat or her cunt or her arse—or taking it from her, with ropes and teeth and finger-nails, with that feather duster whapping red welts against his back while he screamed.

And Kay had even—Mik lurched toward his desk drawer, yanked it open—given him his own. A feather duster. Virtually identical to hers, down to the polished rounded handle, and the switch hidden in the clump of fluffy soft feathers. A little like his Kay, in fact, deceptively innocuous on the outside, with multiple thrilling possibilities hidden within.

Gods, Mik missed her, and in the growing list of things he hadn't understood, this one was beginning to tower above the rest. Having Kay there, waiting, at home, *his*, had been part of what had made everything else easy. It had given him confidence, certainty, the truth that there was always someone there, somewhere to fall. Someone to catch him, to understand him, to *love* him, whenever he needed it.

He was thinking now of when he'd received word that his father had passed, last year. The arsehole's heart had given out in a gaming den, of all places, and with the news there had already been whispers of the debts, the question of whether the estate might be lost, and his family left homeless and impoverished. And that day, Mik had listened to as much as he could from his father's man—his father's *friend*, the bastard—

and then he had turned around, and walked out, and rode straight home, as fast as he could. Not to his mother or Lea, he could admit, but to Kay.

They'd gone at it all night, hurling it back and forth, and Mik couldn't ever remember being in such a state, before or since. Until Kay had tied him standing spread-eagled against the end of his four-poster bed, facing toward it, his wrists lashed to the top of the tall posts, his feet against the bottom.

"You only get to become a lord at my say-so," she'd said, kneeling naked on the bed before him, her eyes flashing in the candlelight, her feather duster trailing against his sweaty, heaving bare chest. "That rubbish-dump of a man who fathered you has nothing whatsoever to do with it. You *earn* your lordship. From *me.*"

Mik had mumbled a helpless denial, and in reply she'd given an insolent glance at that feather duster, rising up between them—and suddenly it had slapped Mik across the face, and then whirled around, and shoved its hard, rounded end deep between his lips. "You *earn* your lordship, Mikkal Mastersson," she'd repeated, her eyes dark and authoritative, her tall body radiating truth and a secret, damning power. "Now show me what you're made of."

And thus had commenced a shocking, impossible beating, swarmed with the deepest agony Kay had ever inflicted on him, studded all through with pleasure unlike anything he'd felt in his life. Rope burns, the whip striking so hard it drew blood, the slick oiled end of the feather duster driving itself bit by bit deep into his heaving body, into his very soul.

She'd forbidden him to come throughout, leaving his dick untouched and screaming, and it hadn't been until the end, when she'd stood wide above him at the end of the bed, with his face desperately sobbing and sucking and slurping between her spread legs, that she'd buried her hands in his hair, tilted his wet face up, and said it.

"Very well, Mikkal Mastersson," she'd said. "I hereby bequeath you the title of Lord Ryning, lord of Ryning Manor, and sole owner of all its wealth and lands."

And with Mik still shaking, staring, she'd sunk to her knees before him, gripped his prick, once—and he'd screamed as he'd sprayed out, spurting strings of thick white liquid all over Kay's waiting body. Marking her belly, her breasts, even her face with his brand-new lord-seed, bequeathed by *her*, and somehow she'd seemed to know what that meant, and had slipped her hands into it, sliding slick against her skin. Painting herself in it, baptizing herself, drawing its power for her own. His witch, his supplicant, his goddess.

Afterwards, once she'd cleaned them both up all over, Mik had finally felt calm again, centred again. And he'd held Kay in his bed, their arms and legs all tangled together, and finally, he'd spoken truth.

"I'm glad he's gone," he'd said, his voice cracking. "I'm so fucking *happy* he's dead. And what kind of lord does that make me?"

But Kay had pulled herself up over him, met his eyes in the guttering candlelight. "It makes you a far better lord than he ever was," she'd told him, her voice firm in its quiet certainty. "You can do this, Mik. You *will*."

And she'd truly believed that. She'd believed in him. She'd given him that night, that true, glorious source of his new lordship, a memory that would without question follow him all his life.

And in return? He'd thrown that away. Trampled it underfoot. Made her *disposable*, and himself into a lord that was perhaps just like his father, after all.

And with the feather duster still in his hands, Mik finally sank back to the bed, covered his eyes, and wept.

9

Mik didn't leave his room until the next morning, when a loud, repeated knock finally had him lurching off the bed, and over to open the door.

Behind it was the tall, blond form of Regin Agmund, one of Mik's fellow air-mages. Regin was legitimately brilliant, one of the few mages in the country who could consistently hit targets with lightning, and thanks to that, he'd become legitimately famous, too. Even so, he was generally a decent fellow, and Mik had always considered him a friend—though now he wasn't so sure, and eyed Regin warily through the half-open door. "What do you want?"

In reply Regin shrugged, and jerked his head at the corridor behind him. "Wanna go for a walk?"

It wasn't the worst idea, seeing how Mik had been brooding alone in his room for the better part of an entire day, so he nodded, grabbed his coat, and accompanied Regin out of Coven Manor, toward the thick forest just beyond the grounds. Earning more narrow-eyed glances from their fellow mages as they passed, but no outright bullshit, and Mik couldn't help a grudging gratefulness to Regin for this, letting himself be seen in public with a shamed lord-turned-pauper.

"Wanna do some drills, then?" Regin asked, once they'd reached their usual training spot, a big open clearing surrounded by trees. A far enough distance away from Coven Manor that the occasional lightning bolt or rain torrent wouldn't alarm anyone, or upset the grounds' careful gardeners.

"Sure," Mik said, and already the clouds were gathering above, at only a glance of Regin's blue eyes. "Thanks."

Regin only shrugged, raised a hand, whipped the storm higher—while across from him Mik rolled up his sleeves, pulled in a deep breath, raised both his hands, and reached for the sky. Using his own magic to try and break Regin's storm, first one way and then another. Dissipate the heat, shove the air up, flatten out the header that Regin was building again and again and again.

They'd drilled like this together for years now, Regin trying to cast and Mik trying to hold him off, mostly because Regin was so strong that most other exercises were useless. But at least this way, Mik got to work and plan and puzzle out possibilities, think on his feet to come up with the most unexpected ways to disarm Regin's ridiculous brute strength.

Today, though, Regin didn't feel quite as overpowering as usual, and it was a good quarter-hour before their first tussle ended, with Regin's inevitable lightning bolt scorching a tree across the clearing. Prompting Mik to give a searching, sidelong look as Regin waved the storm off, his blond head tilted up at the sky.

"Are you going easy on me?" Mik asked suspiciously, but Regin only shrugged, his hand already gathering a new storm above them.

"Nah," he replied. "Magic's just been a bit finicky lately. Ready for another one? Get your sorry arse kicked again?"

Mik nodded, and gave what was probably a pathetic smile back. This was without question the most relaxed he'd felt in days, after the ongoing disaster that had become his life, and as he focused his attention again on the gathering clouds above, he could feel Regin's eyes still on him, studying him.

"So are you really losing everything, then?" Regin asked abruptly, and though maybe Mik should have kept up the farce, he suddenly just felt tired, and resigned, and desperately lonely.

"No," he said, with a sigh. "Not that I'm rolling in coin, by any stretch, but I'll muddle through all right."

A glance at Regin showed his head tilted, his eyebrows raised. "Really?" he asked. "Why'd you let on that you're headed for the poorhouse, then? Not a good look, in a place like this."

He jerked his head back in the direction of Coven Manor, and Mik sighed again, shot him an uncertain, uneasy glance. Regin was the opposite of poor, what with being quite possibly the world's most famous air-mage, but he wasn't from nobility, and hadn't had an Academy education, either. Despite that, he still always had girls falling all over him, though lately he'd settled down with Greta, one of their more unpretentious fellow air-mages, a beautiful blonde heiress who Ilsa incidentally hated.

"I wanted to see what Ilsa would do," Mik replied, finally, and across from him Regin gave a hard, knowing bark of laughter.

"Ah, gold-digger hunting," he said flatly. "Been there, done that. One time I spent an entire month telling girls I had incurable sores on my dick, and that I'd burned through all my coin trying to get them fixed."

Mik couldn't help a choked little chuckle, despite himself. "And did it work?"

"Not enough," Regin replied, frowning back at the

gathering storm above. "Even having a steady girlfriend barely works. It's not easy when people don't like you for *you*."

Mik nodded, his attention only half on the storm now. "Until a few days ago, I thought people *did* like me," he said, with a grimace. "Feeling pretty stupid right about now. Even Ketill threatened to get rid of me."

Regin's gaze dropped back toward Mik, his forehead furrowing. "He did?" he asked, but then a sudden, amused understanding crossed his eyes. "Right. That awful moment when the gold-digger hunting starts working on the higher-ups, too. Go straighten him out, he'll settle down."

But the reality of that still rankled, backed by another one of those uneasy, unnerving realizations that had been plaguing Mik these past days. "But Ketill even saying that, it means," he began, and had to take a breath, make himself continue. "It means I'm only here for my money, my title. I'm not"—he swallowed, met Regin's eyes—"a brilliant mage, really. Am I?"

Regin regarded him for an instant too long, and gods, Mik couldn't bear to hear him say it, so he just kept plowing on, the words tumbling from his mouth. "I taught that seminar yesterday, and some of the kids were utter rubbish, I had no idea how bad—but they're rich and titled, so they get through just fine. Just like me. And there's this girl at home, she's absolutely fucking *brilliant*, way more than I'll ever be, she's an earth-mage but she can even break my *shields*—but there's not a chance in the world she'd ever get into a place like this. And I—I never really stopped to think about how it worked, or paid attention, I bought into our self-serving bullshit hook line and sinker, and now—now—"

He had to bite his lip, clench his hands, because gods, he was on the verge of bawling again, right here, right now, in front of the world's most famous air-mage. To which said air-mage huffed a heavy sigh, and after another moment's silence,

Mik felt a sharp, companionable flick of air, brushing against his shoulder.

"Listen, Mik," Regin said. "I like you, so I'll be honest. You *are* a good mage. You're quick, you've got a light touch, you think on your feet. Of all the air-mages in this place, you're one of the best. But"—Regin sighed, kicked at a rock with his foot—"yeah. Without your title, you probably wouldn't be here. Just like most of these guys. Sorry."

He did look sorry, actually, like he knew just how fucked up that was, that somebody like Mik—or worse, like Kass—got to take up a place at a facility like this, when there were actual brilliant mages like Kay out there, being kept out. And suddenly Mik just felt empty all through, like the colours around him had faded, like all the world had turned grey and hollow.

"Thing is, though," Regin's voice continued, rather quickly, "you're a decent guy, Mik. You're good to have around, good to work with. There are other reasons for keeping somebody on, beyond just skill."

But he was just pitying Mik, at this point, and Mik heard himself give a hard, brittle laugh. "Thanks," he said, "but actually, I know I'm not a decent guy. I'm a slimy, self-absorbed piece of shit, Regin, and I've been coasting through life on my title and my so-called money. You want to know what set all this off, this week? I was home, and I had a huge falling out with my housemaid, who's gorgeous and fucking *brilliant*, and who's finally leaving my sorry arse for good to become an artist, because I've been taking advantage of her for the past ten fucking *years*."

Regin's eyebrows were halfway up his forehead by this point, and the storm above them had faded to just some grey clouds, skidding across the sky. "That the same girl, then?" he asked. "The earth-mage?"

"Yeah," Mik said, voice flat, eyes back up on the clouds overhead. "She specializes in textiles and brushes, you should see what she can come up with, it's incredible. People from all over are trying to buy her stuff, and meanwhile I've kept her trapped with me, in my house, so I can have her whenever the hell I want. Like my *possession*."

He could feel Regin's eyes still on him, and a sideways glance showed him looking disbelieving, and maybe angry, too. "So what, you forced yourself on her, or some shit?" he demanded. "And imprisoned her there? Or *threatened* her, somehow?"

The words were unsettling enough, wrong enough, that Mik recoiled, felt the air twitch around him. "No!" he said, too loud. "No, gods no. I mean, we grew up together, right? My mother hired her after she had my little sister, to help out around the house, when I was maybe fourteen. And I wasn't at school, my mother was busy with the baby, my father was always gone, we were the only kids our age on the estate. So we became—friends. Best friends."

Regin was still watching, still with his eyebrows raised, so Mik just kept talking, getting it out. "We were always teasing each other, always trying to find time to spend together, getting in each other's space. You know? And she was always drawing pictures, and saying they were awful, so I framed one, and put it in my room. And she was embarrassed, and wanted me to take it down, so I told her I only would if she made me a better one. And she did, but she still didn't like it, so on her birthday I took her with me to a painting class, and I was so awful at it that she laughed the whole time, and actually felt comfortable enough to keep going in my place, once I told her I'd paid for them all up front."

Regin was looking nonplussed at this point, and maybe a little impatient, too. "So where does the trapping and forcing come in, again?"

Mik made a face, let out a slow sigh. "Well, things just went from there, you know? We were always together, fooling around, and it just—kept going. And we started playing games with it, teasing each other in that, too, and then *that* kept going, and getting into some pretty intense places, and it"—he gave an awkward shrug—"it kind of ruined me, I think, for the more regular stuff. For regular girls. And I haven't been able to give it up, give *her* up, ever since. And believe me"—he let out another heavy breath—"I've tried."

Regin's expression had shifted back toward disbelief, though his eyebrows were still high on his forehead. "What kind of intense places?" he asked, and Mik felt his face oddly heating, even as the hunger flared, deep in his gut.

"Like—punishing each other," he said finally, with a wince. "Ordering each other around. Playing games like a lord and his maid. Using whips and ropes, that kind of thing."

And damn Regin, because his mouth was hanging open, his eyes staring at Mik with very clear skepticism. "*Really?*"

"Yes, really," Mik snapped back, and for reasons he couldn't quite explain, he yanked down the high collar of his shirt, just enough to show the still-red marks Kay's rope had left on his skin. "Rope burn, three days ago," he said, voice clipped. "And"—he rolled up his sleeve, showed Regin his faintly scarred forearm—"from two months ago. And"—gods, he was losing it, but he reached for his shirt, yanked it up anyway, brandished the faint red splotches on the pale skin of his waist—"candle wax, from a year ago, she accidentally made it *way* too fucking hot."

Mik was smiling a little, even as the ache twisted in his stomach, because Kay had been such a mess over that, and had fussed over him for weeks afterwards. Which Mik had milked for all it was worth, getting multiple very good massages and blow jobs out of the deal, and it had been so good, had always been so good, and *gods* he missed her, so much it hurt.

"So how's that taking advantage again?" Regin asked. "Sounds like a two-way thing to me. Sounds pretty hot, too."

He looked like he actually meant that, eyeing Mik with something almost like a newfound respect, but Mik grimaced again, shaking his head. "She wanted more," he said. "More than being just my mistress. And I couldn't give it."

There was an instant's silence, the look of disbelief back on Regin's face. "Why not?" he asked. "Kinda sounds like a no-brainer, Mik, honestly."

What? Mik blinked at him, and felt that ache churn again in his gut. "Because she's my *housemaid*. Lords don't marry their housemaids."

But Regin only shrugged, and gave an absentminded wave up toward the sky, gathering the clouds again. "Thought you said she left you to become an artist," he said. "What, lords can't marry artists, either?"

Mik blinked again, his mouth opening and closing. *Could* lords marry artists? No, not really, or could they? People might know her past, might comment and whisper and laugh, Mik would be a mockery of a lord—but wait, he already was, wasn't he?

"Or," Regin said, eyeing Mik again, "maybe it's *you* who's not into it, once she's not your servant anymore? Can't get the same kick from it?"

But Mik's heart was oddly jumping, skipping its beats, lurching into double-time. And he gave a distracted shake of his head, because of course he would still want Kay if she wasn't his servant, that was just the tease, just the game. And if she was an artist... could a lord marry an artist... *could* he?

You'd have made me a partner, she'd said, and that's exactly what she'd wanted, wasn't it? A partner, a family, a *husband*? And gods, Mik was a mess again, everything was a mess, but suddenly there was a small pinprick of light, of clarity, of *hope*.

"I need to go," he said, in a voice not his own, as he turned away, aiming for the manor—but then he halted, looking over his shoulder. "Thanks, Regin. You're a good friend. I'll see you around, all right?"

Regin raised an eyebrow, but nodded, and gave a little wave of his hand. Saying farewell, and they both knew it, because Mik nodded back, and ran.

10

I t turned out that disassembling one's life, one's entire career, was a far simpler task than Mik would ever have thought.

It only took one short, deeply satisfying meeting with Ketill, during which he informed Ketill that yes, those unfortunate rumours about the demise of his lordship had been sadly mistaken, and that he was, in fact, leaving Coven Manor to finally assume said lordship full-time.

Ketill had shamelessly tried to backtrack his earlier threats, spouting nonsense about how Mik was one of their best mages, one of the few Regin would agree to work with, and how difficult it would be to find a replacement. Thankfully, Mik was now informed enough to see this for the claptrap it was, and shut Ketill down with a few decisive curses, before striding out of his office forever.

He would have to send a wagon for his things, he knew, but it was no difficult matter to pack it all—including Kay's paintings, carefully wrapped in clothes—into his trunks, which he'd sent for from storage. And by afternoon's end, his room was stripped bare, but for the three trunks standing in the middle of it, and Mik himself.

He spent perhaps a half-hour saying perfunctory goodbyes, not bothering to argue the assumption that he was leaving due to his financial difficulties—because beyond Regin, not a single one of his longtime colleagues had even bothered asking whether the rumours were indeed true. Fixing him instead with sidelong glances that ranged from sympathetic to hostile, and by the end of it Mik was deeply, irrevocably glad to be free of the cursed place for good.

He rode home that evening, pushing Leni far harder than he should have in the dark, but he desperately needed to get there, to get home. To Kay.

He still wasn't quite certain of his full intentions around Kay yet, but there was a deep, grim determination that it would be different. He would do better. He would offer more. He would *listen*.

By the time he rode through his own gates, his heart was pounding so loud he could hear it, and he could scarcely speak to Berin, his groom, who watched with wary, bemused eyes as Mik leapt off Leni's back, and all but sprinted toward the house.

Hallum, the footman, looked just as surprised to see Mik stalking through the front door—and then, even more so, halfway down the stairs in her dressing gown, was Mik's mother. Who broke off her yawn to stare at him, and then clattered down the rest of the stairs at once, and dragged him into her arms.

"What is it, Mikkal?" she demanded. "What's wrong? Why are you back so soon?"

Mik squeezed her tightly, breathing in the familiar flowery smell of her, and then leaned back to meet her eyes. "I quit," he said. "I'm moving home."

And bless his mother, because the look on her face was all warmth and delight, not a single doubt to be seen. "Truly,

Mikkal?" she exclaimed. "Oh, that's wonderful. Such a big deci-
sion, but it will be so lovely to have you home again, we've
missed you so, darling."

She embraced him again, patting his hair as though he
were a child again, and Mik heard himself laugh, perhaps the
first time he'd done so in days. "It was long overdue, Mother,"
he said. "I've missed you, too."

When she pulled away her eyes were bright, and she was
blinking hard, but still smiling. "So what brought on this
sudden change of heart?" she asked. "You were so committed to
your work there."

Mik looked at her, took a breath, let it out. He wanted to
start telling the truth. He wanted to stop being an awful human
being. And he could tell the truth about this. He could.

"Kay," he said, his voice catching, and he could see the
understanding cross his mother's eyes. No judgement, thankfully, but perhaps something else, something...

"Where is she?" Mik asked, and his heart was racing again,
his eyes glancing toward the stars. "In bed?"

But his mother's mouth was opening and closing, her eyes
blinking again, and Mik felt his elation plummet, all at once.
And before even she spoke, he knew.

"I'm so sorry, Mikkal," she said. "Kay is gone."

11

Gone. Kay was gone.

Mik squeezed his eyes shut, and fought to block out the sudden dangerous rushing in his head, juddering behind his hands, his heart. Kay couldn't be gone. Not yet. Not now, not when he needed her, *please.*

"Where?" he heard himself ask, his voice not his own. "To her new place?"

He opened his eyes in time to see his mother nodding. "She moved the day after you left," she said. "I don't know her new coordinates. Lea has them, but she's asleep."

Shit, fuck, *damnation.* And even as Mik was deliberating whether to run up and wake Lea, demand that she give him Kay's address this very moment, he also knew very well that Ashon was still a good hour's ride away, it was dark, and Berin already had Leni stabled up for the night. And would Kay even want to see him this late? Would Kay even want to see him at all?

That was another question that had been rising in Mik's thoughts, and it was almost debilitating in its power, in the sheer caustic ruthlessness of it. Maybe Kay didn't want an apology. Maybe they were too far gone. Maybe Mik had fucked this up for good, forever.

Your possession, she'd said. *Disposable.*

His breath was coming too fast and harsh, something white sparking behind his eyes, and he made himself swallow, hard. "I'll go in the morning, then," he said. "But first"—he pulled himself taller, looked his mother in the eye, gathered his courage—"I'd like to have Grandmother's ring. Please."

His mother's shock was visible, rippling against her dressing gown, but she did a creditable job of keeping her outward composure, and twitched a short, unsteady nod. And then she turned, abruptly, and went back up the stairs, leaving Mik to follow along behind.

He hadn't been in his mother's dressing room for months, though it had been a favourite childhood haunt of his, and he knew exactly where she kept the ring, in the little ebony box on the side table. It had been her own mother's ring, and her mother's before her, and its glittering blue sapphire caught the candlelight as his mother handed it over, her fingers slightly trembling.

Mik accepted it in silence, sliding it onto his own little finger for safekeeping, and his mother watched the movement, something convulsing in her throat. "Are you certain, Mikkal?" she said finally, her voice hoarse. "I mean—of course I do not begrudge you marrying for affection, and I know there is a special bond between you, but—"

Mik raised his eyebrows at her, waiting, and she sighed, sank heavily down onto the nearest chair. "People will talk, Mikkal. It will always shadow you. It will affect your future prospects, your relationships with your peers. Some people will refuse to associate with you over it. Or worse."

But Mik had just endured several deeply enlightening days with said two-faced peers, and jerked a hard shake of his head. "I've spent a lot of time thinking these past days," he replied.

"And I have come to realize that I care very little for what they think. These are the people"—he felt his lip curl—"who associated with my father, who approved of my father, despite knowing what he did to you, to us. If they refuse to associate with me over loving someone supposedly beneath me, then they are not worth my regard, or my time."

His mother was watching him very closely, eyes searching his—but then her mouth slowly, gently, curved up into a wan, watery smile. And in an instant she was embracing Mik again, sniffing into his shoulder. "Very well, my son," she said. "You are wiser than your years."

Mik should have disabused her of that notion, but perhaps it was well enough to leave it there, and after a brief kiss to her hair, and a quiet murmured thank-you, he said goodnight, and made for his own bedroom. Which was precisely as he had left it, down to—he hesitated, and stepped toward the mantel—the silent, innocuous-looking feather duster.

Mik exhaled as he looked, reached out a slow finger to touch. And then he spun on his heel, not for the bed, but for the writing desk. *Lords don't write their housemaids*, Kay had said, and so Mik lit a candle, pulled out a clean sheet of paper, dipped the quill in the ink.

Dearest Kay, he wrote, and then sat back, and looked at it. His heartbeat was whirling up again, the twist in his gut tightening dangerously, how was he supposed to say this, what in the hell could possibly make ten years right again.

There was nothing that could, really, so Mik took a hard, fortifying breath, and put the quill back to the paper. And for perhaps the first time, he faced down the bare truth of all this, in stark black and white.

You were right, he wrote, slow, careful. *You were right, and I didn't listen, because I didn't want to hear it. I didn't want to believe that you had options beyond me. A life beyond me.*

His eyes were prickling, but he took another breath, kept

writing. *If I had believed that, of course I would have had to face the truth that our arrangement was unfair to you. I would have had to face how I was truly treating you. I would have had to see you as a real person, with goals and wishes of your own, rather than simply my possession.*

I see now what I have done, he wrote. *I wish I could go back, and change my actions. I wish I had been a better friend to you, a better man. I wish I had found a better way. I am so sorry.*

He signed the letter with his signet ring, dipped in ink, and then his first name, just to make it clear. And then blew on it, rolled it up, tied it tight. And sat there to wait, alone, until dawn.

12

Morning finally came, slowly but inevitably, finding Mik exactly where night had left him. Sitting in that damned chair, staring at that damned letter, and twisting his mother's ring on his finger.

He hadn't bothered trying to sleep—he was in far too much of a state at this point—and he finally stood, stretching his creaky joints. And then he grabbed for his satchel, and put the letter—and, after a moment's hesitation, the abandoned feather duster—inside it.

Next was to wake Lea—he didn't feel quite so guilty doing it now, though it was still early—and after knocking loudly and repeatedly at her door, he finally earned himself a mumbled admittance, and the comical sight of Lea sitting up in bed, with her hair all in curling papers, her bleary blue eyes blinking owlishly toward him.

"Mik?" she said. "Why're you here again? Is something wrong?"

Mik went to sit on the bed, tried to smile. "Well," he replied, "I quit my job."

"What?!" Lea shrieked, and immediately hurled her

nightgown-clad form toward him, squeezing her slim arms around his shoulders. "You mean it? For good? You're moving back in? Forever?!"

Mik nodded, felt his smile become a twitch more genuine. "You see the good side now," he told her, as lightly as he could manage, "but just wait until we're fighting over desserts, or I'm casting frantic air-spells at shadows, or I become an excessively virtuous matron who looms and grunts at every boy who so much as looks at you."

But Lea only gave a delighted laugh, a sharp elbow in Mik's side. "It'll be *fun*," she replied. "I'm so *glad*, Mik. It's so lonely here sometimes with only me and Mother. Especially now that Kay's gone, too."

Her eyes had darkened, and Mik took a slow, shaky breath. "About that," he said, carefully. "Mother says you have her new coordinates?"

Lea promptly nodded, and began digging through the mess of papers and books on her nightstand. "Here," she said, "though wait, I'd better copy it, it's my only one."

So Mik accordingly waited while she wrote it out again, and then handed it over. And as Mik took it from her, her eyes suddenly narrowed, and she grasped for his hand, holding it toward the window's brightening light.

She was looking at the ring on his pinky finger, and then blinked up at his face. "Mik," she gasped. "You're *not*."

But Mik could only seem to shrug, his eyes trapped on her face. What would she think, what would she say—but suddenly here was the smile, splitting her face in two, brightening the entire room. "You *are*!" she crowed. "I knew it! Especially after you found out she was leaving, you turned into an *ogre*, Mik! It's just like a fairy tale!"

Mik couldn't help a choked laugh, shaking his head at her. "Me turning into an ogre is the opposite of a fairy tale, Lea," he said. "It's the very stuff of nightmares, actually. And even if Kay agrees"—he swallowed—"it might affect how people see us. How people treat us. Even *you*, munchkin."

He hated to say it, true as it was, but Lea only gave a dismissive toss of her curl-papered head. "I don't care what people think of me," she replied, "and you shouldn't either. Besides, Kay's so lovely, as soon as they meet her they'll all just be jealous, and you'll be fine again."

She fixed him with her most winning smile, as though she'd solved all the world's problems at once, and Mik grinned back this time, and tousled his hand—carefully—against the curl-papered hair. "Thanks, munchkin," he said. "I'll let you know how it goes."

Lea kept smiling beatifically toward him as he left, like there was no possible way any of this could go wrong, but as Mik clattered down the stairs toward the stable, he knew better. He'd fucked this up. Badly. And if Kay didn't want to forgive him, didn't want to even see him, he had to accept it. She was a real person. She had the right to decide her own life.

He once again rode poor Leni far too hard toward Ashon, toward the address Lea had given him. It turned out to be a little whitewashed cottage, slightly beyond the edge of town, and surrounded by tall oaks and firs. It looked like just the kind of place Kay would choose, and Mik slowed Leni to a walk as they approached, and then stopped altogether, and tied Leni off to a tree. And then just stood there staring at the cottage, feeling his palms go sweaty, his heart thumping erratically in his chest. Kay was here.

And he knew she was here, because the door and windows were all wide open, and that meant she was painting, just there, inside. And finally Mik made himself lurch forward, one step and then another, and gods it felt like he was walking through mud, and also, like he was going to sick up all over his boots.

He somehow made it to the open door, and raised a hand to knock on the wooden frame—but there, just visible inside it, was Kay. Standing across the room with her back to the door, and a huge canvas in front of her. It was another landscape, another view from Mik's lands, and—his throat closed off— there was another rainstorm, gathering in the far corner.

The brushes were dipping and flying all around her, five or six moving all at once, and she was wearing another old tunic—another one of Mik's old tunics, in fact—and a pair of slim, paint-spattered trousers. Her hair was in its perfect neat bun, but her feet were bare, and gods, Mik just wanted to look, and look, and look.

But he had to clear his throat, to breathe, and at the sudden noise Kay whirled around to face him. And he could see the colour drain from her face all at once, could see how the brushes trembled in midair before falling to bounce against the paint-spattered drop cloth below.

"Mik," she whispered, and even the sound of her voice almost made him gasp, made him have to briefly close his eyes, fight for air. And then look again, had to see her again, hold this vision in his mind, no matter what she said or did.

"I—" he began, his voice rough, and his shaky hands groped for his satchel, tugging the clasp open. "I wrote you"— he held it out, his hand wavering—"a letter."

He could see Kay swallow, her eyes held uneasy to the white scroll, but she carefully stepped closer on the drop cloth, and took it. Unfurling it before her with only a look—she was just as good with paper as she was with cloth and brushes— and silently began to read.

It didn't take long, as it wasn't a long letter, and when it was done her eyes snapped back to Mik, searching, strange. But she wasn't speaking, and that meant this was on him, it was all on him, he had to pull himself together, speak the truth.

"I'm so sorry," he said, his voice cracking. "I truly am. I didn't want to see what I was doing to you. I didn't want to accept that you might not"—his voice cracked again—"need me."

Kay was still silent, still staring, in this moment not a witch or a goddess or a supplicant or a maid or even an artist—but just *her*. And Mik felt his gut fighting to buckle, the truth too raw to bear, to breathe.

"But I need you, Kay," he said. "I love you. And you said you wanted a family, and a partner, and a better answer, from me. So please, my love"—he staggered to his knees on the drop cloth, held up the sapphire ring—"marry me."

13

It was like the room had turned to stone around Mik, with Kay the only life left in it. Standing stock-still, staring at him, and on the floor the brushes all seemed to rumble at once, or perhaps that was the actual earth, twitching beneath Mik's knees.

"But," she said, the word a single breathing whisper, rasping out her frozen mouth. "But you—you said—you said I *can't.* You said that woman isn't me. You've said it for years, Mik, *years,* this is some kind of joke, a trick, a—"

Her chest was heaving, as if the breath was too faint to catch, and suddenly Mik felt just the same, like the room had been sucked dry of all its air. "I know I said it," he managed. "I know. But it was an awful thing to say, it was cruel to you, and it wasn't even *true.* It was my own stupid fucking rule, and I only made it because my head was too far up my arse to see what I had in front of me."

His voice had gone hard and bitter at the end, and suddenly he couldn't bear to look at Kay anymore, and dropped his eyes to the spatters of paint around her feet. "I made you feel disposable," his hollow voice said. "Replaceable. Like you were only a possession, a plaything. But in truth, Kay"—he winced, rubbed his eyes—"you are the least disposable thing in my life. You're the one thing I can't live without. I can't sleep, I can't remember the last time I've eaten, I can't *breathe* but for thoughts of you. I keep obsessing over your paintings and your fucking *feather dusters* and every terrible thing I've ever said and done to you—"

His voice broke, his eyes threatening to drip the wetness that was rapidly pooling behind them. "I was so awful to you," he gulped. "I should have treasured you, and cherished you. I should have shown you how much you meant to me. And I should never, ever have even *looked* at anyone else but you. It was selfish, and thoughtless, and cruel—and so fucking *stupid*, because none of them ever measured up to you, ever. You didn't deserve it, Kay. You deserved so, so much better."

His mouth threatened to crumple, and he rubbed his stinging eyes, shook his head. "I can't even promise to be a good husband to you," he said, his voice barely audible. "Because I do still want you to be all my own, I want to have you and keep you in every way there is. I want to make you my family and have you live in my house and bear my children, and in all that, I'm still going to want you to whip me, and deep-throat me, and pretend that my magic is as good as yours. I *did* make you suit me, Kay, and now there's no one else in the world who *does*."

There was still the stilted frozen silence, hovering above him, and Mik made his eyes blink up, made himself ignore the streak of wetness slipping down his cheek. "But here I am, talking again," he said, to Kay's staring, still eyes. "Not listening. And I want to listen, Kay. I want to hear what *you* think."

Kay's body twitched again, her face so deathly pale, and her mouth opened, and closed. And opened again, and he heard her try to draw in breath, dragging ragged through her chest.

"But—" she whispered, and then her eyes squeezed shut. "But my *work*, Mik."

Mik opened his mouth to reply to that, to blurt out whatever promises she wanted to hear—but then closed it again. Waiting, listening, because she wasn't done, and he had to give her that space, no matter how much it would hurt, in the end.

"I just moved here," she said, still not looking at him, her voice so tenuous, so—*desperate*, somehow. "I just accepted four new commissions, I'm finally making my own life, and—"

It was like the world had plunged beneath Mik, dropping him into its depths, and he had to sit back on his heels, twist that ring back onto his shaking finger, fight to swallow the sudden choking misery in his throat. She wanted her life. Not his. And she deserved that, she did, and he fucking deserved it, too.

He should have left, then, taken the words for the truth they were, the truth he'd asked for. But he couldn't seem to move, suddenly, couldn't even lift his head, and he just sat there, staring at Kay's bare feet, while the wetness streaked down his face. Kay didn't want him. Kay didn't need him anymore. She was done.

But then there was a strange sound from above him, and when Mik's wet eyes looked up, Kay was—weeping. Not just regretful, not just a sad goodbye, but full-on dragged-out *anguish*, coming out of her in gasping, heaving sobs, shaking her shoulders, breaking through her quivering hands over her mouth.

And Mik stared, and tried to think, because he wasn't fucking *listening*, again. And he staggered up to his unsteady feet, and watched his trembly hand come up, brushing at the wetness on Kay's face. Watched her sobs hitching, breaking, as her head tilted immediately, almost desperately, into the touch of his fingers.

"I know you want your own life, love," he heard himself say, hoarse. "But can't I be part of that?"

Kay's whole body stilled again, her eyes again frozen on his, and Mik kept his fingers sliding gentle on her face, feeling his way. "Of course you need to keep painting," he whispered. "And accepting commissions, and doing your work here, if that's what you want. But you said you wanted a family too, and can't"—he took another shaky, thick breath—"can't that be me?"

Kay's eyes fluttered, her breath catching, and in that instant, suddenly, it was like the world had snapped back into place under Mik's feet again. Because that meant she wanted it. She wanted it, just as much as he did, and he just had to wait, to listen, to *understand*.

"Because," she replied, finally, "your—your work, Mik. We'd still—be apart, so often, especially if I'm here, and you're there, it's even further than before, and I miss you so desperately when you're gone, and it's so *awful* when you leave again, and all those other well-born accomplished girls are there and it's just—it's just easier—safer—to—"

She gave a frantic little wave at the room around her, and suddenly Mik did understand, and gods, why hadn't he listened before? "Kay," he said, and he put both his hands to her face now, cradling it, making her look at him. "I quit. Yesterday. I'm moving home."

Kay's shock was palpable, jolting against his hands, and he saw the disbelief fill her eyes, briefly crowding out the misery. "What?" she croaked. "*Why?*"

But she was with him, suddenly, somehow, something changed in her eyes, and Mik felt that earth beneath him, the air around him, his Kay's face in his hands. "Because," he heard himself say, soft, "you are a *witch*, Kay. And you sent me away under an appalling spell of enlightenment that dropped all the scales from my eyes at once, and made me realize that my life is utter *hell* without you."

And there it was, the reluctant little twitch at the corner of her mouth, so Mik came a short step closer, let himself breathe in the succulent, familiar scent of her. "If I had stayed away any longer," he murmured, "I'm sure I would have succumbed to madness permanently, locked away alone with your feather duster. Thus was the strength of your spell."

There was another twitch of Kay's mouth, showing a hint of dimple this time, and Mik tilted her face up, held her still-wet eyes. "I am utterly at your mercy, witch," he whispered. "What fresh hell will you visit upon me next?"

Kay's breath hitched, but her eyes on him were unmistakably warm, even as they brimmed with fresh tears. "Oh, you have no *idea*, your lordship," she said, her voice cracking. "I've been lying in wait for years, anticipating this very moment."

The gasp from Mik's throat came out more like a sob, because it had to mean—maybe. It had to mean his Kay was considering it, truly, and it was a revelation, a miracle, a gift from his benevolent beautiful goddess, a curse from his powerful witch, a promise, a hope of a whole new *life*.

And it was consuming him, suddenly, his entire body twitching and trembling with the strength of it. Doing its damnedest to break him, but no, no, that was Kay's job, and Mik let out a ragged, high-pitched moan at the thrilling, gut-wrenching feeling of a rope, snaking its way up his back.

"Your many misdeeds," Kay's voice said, breathy but suddenly sure of itself, of him, "may be forgiven you. If you prove yourself man enough, lord enough, to accept your justly deserved punishment."

Mik frantically nodded, even as the rope curled up over his shoulder, circling close and safe around his neck. Rubbing harsh against the rope burn she'd left last time, but it felt good, so fucking good, and Mik's dick in his trousers had already flooded with heat, straining to escape.

And Kay knew it, of course she did, and with a single, disdainful glance from her eyes, Mik's clothes tore themselves off his skin entirely, peeling away in pieces behind him.

Leaving him naked and exposed and wholly vulnerable, with that rope tight around his neck, and his swollen cock jutting and twitching toward her.

He could see her eyeing it, her own breath catching hard in her throat—but then she lifted her eyes, angling them to something above him. And it was another rope, sliding over the cottage's exposed rafter above, while—Mik groaned—the other end of the rope had already come to wrap around his right wrist, and yanked it up, hard. And then it snapped to grasp the other wrist, wrapping them tight together, both now bound and pulled tight, straight above Mik's head.

The next rope came for his right ankle, yanking it out sideways, and then tying its other end around one of the cottage's thick wooden support joists, rising from the floor to the ceiling. And then another rope did the same to Mik's other ankle in the other direction, pulling him almost precariously off-balance, and when he found his footing again, it was on straining, spread-apart legs, his arms tied firmly above, that rope still firmly around his neck.

And Kay. His witch, his goddess. Standing oh so innocently before him, still dressed in her painting clothes, her head tilting in something almost like amusement. "Are you comfortable, my lord?"

"No," Mik's mouth immediately replied, because this was definitely deeply uncomfortable, his legs already trembling, his shoulders cramping. "This is absolute torment, witch, and you could at least shut the fucking door."

The door was indeed still wide open to the outdoors, and though Mik's strung-up body perhaps wouldn't be visible to a casual passerby's first glance, anyone directly approaching the door would certainly, unquestionably see him. A lord, tied up and spread-eagled, held entirely at his witch's command.

His magic could have easily dealt with it, of course, but he was accepting his punishment, caught in his witch's thrall. And she saw it, she *approved*, and her mouth twitched up as the rope around Mik's neck jerked back, hard enough to rattle his teeth in his mouth.

"I said," repeated her cool voice, "are you comfortable, my lord?"

Oh gods, and Mik pulled in a gasping, thick breath. "Yes," he heard himself say. "Very much so, my lady."

The smile tugged a little wider, showing a hint of sharp teeth, and one of Kay's still-wet paintbrushes snapped up off the floor, and into her waiting hand. Twirling once in her fingers, and then reaching out to brush gentle against Mik's heaving chest, dabbing him with a spot of wet, slippery whiteness.

"Better," she murmured, as she began a slow, torturous circle around Mik's exposed body, lightly trailing her brush against him as she went. Painting him with a thick white line all around, feeling cool and prickly against his bare skin, and he shivered all over as she did it again, again, looping the brush lower each time.

"This isn't punishment, witch," he heard his perverse voice say, between gasps, as the brush hovered over to dip itself in fresh paint, and then floated back, now drawing a slow, torturous line down the shaft of his aching, straining prick. "This is just you adding a very long bath to my day's busy to-do list."

There was a hiss of disapproval from Kay's mouth, that cool wet brush circling against the leaking head of him, nudging white paint under his skin. "Your day's to-do list," she said, "involves only me, and my retribution, and your long-overdue penitence."

With that, the brush that had been painting him, caressing him, whirled itself around, and scraped its thin pointed handle sharp and painful across Mik's waist. Making him twitch all over, his white-painted cock jerking frantically, and in front of him Kay raised an eyebrow, as the brush's pointed tip began sliding in slow, threatening circles, moving lightly up his skin.

"What do you say, my lord?" she asked, as another brush rose up behind her, this one far larger, its wooden handle nearly the width of a broomstick. "Will you beg for my leniency?"

Mik's mouth laughed, his head thrown back, taunting her, meeting her in it. "Never," he drawled. "Nothing you can do will make me beg you, witch, *ever*."

But he had been on his knees begging not even a half-hour before, and would do so again in a heartbeat. And he saw that certainty flare across Kay's eyes, saw truth and satisfaction and perhaps even a grim, grateful rage.

"Very well, my lord," she said, voice calm, remote. "You asked for it."

And before Mik could blink, or breathe, the huge handle of that brush had whirled around, and struck him across the cheek. Not enough to leave lasting damage, but still hard enough to make his eyes water, to bring an unwilling gasp to his mouth.

"Wench," he growled, but the smaller brush only scraped again, sharp as a fingernail, all the way down his torso, while the other brush's thick wooden handle shoved up under his chin. Pushing his head back, exposing his bare neck, his throat desperately swallowing against the tightening twist of Kay's rope.

It was a deeply uncomfortable position, one that made him have to strain to even see Kay, who was—Mik gasped again—raising up even more brushes into the air around her. Large brushes, small brushes, wet brushes, dry brushes, all spinning slowly around her, hovering and menacing, as if listening, watching, awaiting her command.

And then, with a wave of her hand, a toss of her blonde head—they *attacked*. Swarming toward Mik all at once, giving him only enough warning to close his eyes, his whole body clenching tight—before they were on him, furious and frantic. Beating and scraping and whipping against his skin, clawing at him like frantic flying beasts, pain blooming and whirling in their wake.

Mik choked and strained against them, fighting to escape, but there was no escape, no recourse. Only the powerful, spinning strikes of the larger brushes, already deeply painful as they made new bruises, rang against bone. And the shrill, screeching scrapes of the smaller brushes, drawing red patterns on his skin, and beyond that, above that, the cool soft wet slide of the paint-covered brushes as they covered him, explored him, marked him as Kay's own. On his nipples, across his cheeks, slow and torturous down between his legs and underneath, all the way back up his crease.

His legs were shaking badly at this point, but he was accepting this, he deserved this, even as he felt another hard handle—a suspiciously slick-feeling metal one—gently slide against his crease, searching, circling, delving. And then finding what it had come for, oh gods oh fuck, Mik's entire body fighting and straining and enduring as he was pierced, breached, split apart.

It had to be huge, bigger than anything she'd used on him before, and he heard his voice keening as it pressed, sank deeper. As the rest of the brushes kept pelting all around, clawing and striking his skin, and another slim metal one— Mik shouted, fought and failed to wrench away—delved softly, but purposefully, in front, against his open, leaking slit.

Kay had only done that once or twice before, when they'd both been very still and clean and careful, and while it had been hot as fuck, it was also thoroughly, abjectly terrifying. And the threat of it here, now, with Mik's entire body filthy and trembling and on fire, was more than enough to shock him stock-still, even as that hard brush handle kept driving in deeper and deeper in behind him, breaking him apart, holy mother of *fuck*.

"Wait," he heard himself gasp, and thank the gods, the pressure against his prick eased off, just slightly. And so did the rest of the brushes too, now hovering threateningly in midair all around him, except for that one behind him, still buried halfway up inside him, fuck, *fuck*.

"Yes, my lord?" Kay asked, cool and disdainful, for all the world a force of malevolence, of utter unearthly power. And gods curse her, but that slim brush handle against his slit delved again, just slightly, and a glance down at it was almost Mik's undoing, his straining ruddy prick pointing straight out toward her, with *that* pointing straight out of it, and ending in a wet, dripping brush-tip, held lightly in Kay's paint-stained fingers.

Mik couldn't breathe, couldn't drag his eyes away, even as he felt that hardness move again behind him, sinking deeper, stronger, everywhere, everything. About to conquer him from all sides, break him in two, pain still radiating everywhere else, blood or paint or both, dripping down his chest and his back and his legs—and suddenly he was lost, broken, empty.

"My lord?" Kay's cool voice said again, dragging his eyes up to it, to her face. His witch, his supplicant, his goddess, his captor, his deliverance, and Mik gave a frantic, helpless shake of his head. He couldn't, couldn't face it, or her, the words weren't there. And suddenly the game had somehow broken, vanished, trailing away in wisps through his grasping empty fingers.

"Kay," he croaked, and he saw her eyes change, shifting from the witch to the supplicant to something else entirely. "You—you still haven't *said*."

Kay's eyes kept changing, witch-goddess-worshipper, and Mik was lost in them, hopeless, wretched. "I'll take anything you want to give," he breathed, "play any way you want. But I—I need to *know*, Kay."

And within a breath, the ropes binding Mik had loosened, snaking themselves off and away from his badly shaking form, and without their support he buckled helplessly down to his hands and knees on Kay's paint-streaked drop cloth. Blinking wet down at his rubbed-raw wrists, his paint-streaked hands, and he opened and closed his numb fingers as his screaming shoulders shuddered with his gasping breaths. Fuck, had he fucked it up, and he finally shoved himself back onto his heels, so he could look at her face.

And Kay looked—appalled. Aghast. Staring at him as though he were a horrifying sight, and perhaps he was, streaked in paint and blood and sweat, his breath heaving, that damned brush handle behind him still locked halfway up inside.

"Please," he said, and he pulled that sapphire ring off his finger again, now rather covered in her paint, and perhaps his own life's blood. "Tell me," he whispered, pleaded. "Will you marry me, Kay."

The world stopped, held, waited on the answer, on her staring shocked eyes. On his penitent, his worshipper, his priestess, falling to her knees before him, and dragging his broken body whole into her arms.

"Yes," she whispered, and the single word was life, surging under Mik's skin. "Oh, Mik, of course. *Yes.*"

14

If there was a single moment in Mik's life he would never, ever forget, it was this one. Kneeling broken and ragged and bloody in Kay's cottage, with a paintbrush half up his arse, and his shaky hand sliding an engagement ring onto his new fiancee's badly trembling finger.

The ring fit, luckily, and Mik held her hand in both of his, eyeing it with a rising, reckless satisfaction. Kay had said *yes*. She was wearing his ring. She was his. *Permanently*.

He felt almost triumphant, suddenly, like a man who'd battled his way through a horde, and finally won his prize. But when he glanced up at Kay's face, she still looked pale and shaken, her eyes locked to their joined hands, to Mik's grandmother's ring on her still-shaking finger.

"You can't really mean it," she whispered, but her eyes were still fixed on it, her other hand brushing careful against the glittering stone. "You *can't*, Mik."

Not that again, and suddenly Mik's own anger flared up, his throat letting out a hard, guttural growl. Like he really was transforming into that ogre, here on his hands and knees, furious and sticky and filthy all over.

"Hell, yes, I can," he hissed at her, and with a harsh sudden movement, a fierce gust of air, he shoved her back onto the drop cloth, leaning powerful and aggressive over her still-clothed body. "I'll do whatever the fuck I want with you, wench. Now, clothes off."

Kay hesitated, blinking up at him like he was something new, strange—but he was, and he hauled her up by the shirt, dragging her staring face closer to his. "I said, clothes *off*!" he roared, more air flaring straight in her face, and thank the gods, she nodded, and complied. Dragging the trousers down, the tunic up, hurling them off her body with surprising force, and under them she was fucking pristine, beautiful and pale and unmarked, the utter opposite of the mess she'd made of Mik's body above her.

"You're *mine* now, witch," Mik growled at her, dropping his hand to grasp hard at her breast, streaking her with his filth. "Mine. *Forever*."

Kay didn't look like she disliked the idea, suddenly, her breast peaked and heaving under the grasp of his hand, so he did the same to the other side, watching with perverse vindication as her pale skin darkened, streaked with him, his own. And he looked at her, and smiled a wicked smile at her, and watched her whole body ripple and shudder in reply.

"Mine," he growled again, as he let his hand trail down her belly, the crease of her hip. And then he shoved her legs apart, not gently, with his own knees, so he could slide his hand up against her silky-slick spread-apart wetness, already dripping, swollen, open, for him.

"And that means," he purred, as he slipped a finger inside, "I finally get to have my way with you, wench. And"—watching her face, he slid in a second finger, deep—"I get to make you take whatever the hell I want. Whether that's my dick, or my whole fucking hand, or my goddamn *children*."

Kay under him gave a helpless, choked gasp, and he slid in a third finger, feeling the tightness of her now, hot slick darkness all around his fingers. And then, still watching her face, he curved those fingers up, rubbing just where he knew she liked it, and gave a hard, satisfied laugh. "And you're damn well going to like it," he continued. "It's going to be everything you ever fucking *dreamed* of, and every morning you're going to get on your knees, and suck my dick down your throat, and *thank* me."

Kay was whimpering helplessly, her body arching against his hand, driving against him, and he kept at it, circling and brushing his fingers again and again and again. "It's going to be so *good*, wench," he breathed, blowing warm heat against her cheek as he felt her go tighter, rigid, clenching closer all around him. "And you'll finally have to behave, and obey me, and be a good proper lord's wife—"

Her release came with a sound not unlike a scream, her body gripping again and again against his delving fingers, and between his own suddenly ragged gasps Mik managed another smug, dark smile. "Note how generous your lord husband will be," he said, "when you please me."

Kay's replying moan was more like a whimper, her body still trembling against him, and Mik slowly slid his dripping wet fingers out, trailed them up her silken skin. Through the streaky mess he'd made, all the way up to her open mouth, where they slipped deep between her parted lips.

She sucked almost immediately, drinking down her own juices with head-swarming eagerness, and Mik smiled again, watched as his fingers slipped deeper between her lips, brushing light against her hot, convulsing throat. "That's a good wife," he whispered. "Now beg me to fuck you."

Kay's whole body arched under him, all lithe pale silken beauty, and even as Mik's dick strained and convulsed to take it, his hand reached over across her, and slid itself into a wet pool of paint that had somehow gotten dumped on the floor.

"I said, beg, wife," he breathed, as he brought his hand back again, trailing his slick, dripping finger against her skin. Drawing up from her waist to her nipple, slightly down and over to the other, giving it a little pinch, and then back down. Leaving the unmistakable shape of an *M* behind, marking her, and for good measure Mik left the rest of the paint in a clear glistening handprint, against the curve of her hip—and then blew it all dry, with another hard flare of air from his mouth.

"Beg, wife," he ordered. "Or I make that"—he nodded at the *M* he'd made—"permanent, while you scream."

That seemed to do it, breaking Kay's blinking eyes from whatever spell they'd been caught under, and she arched up again, finally putting her hands to Mik's slick, sticky back. Stinging as they slid against his various cuts and bruises, but he didn't give a damn, and moved up to lean closer over her, shoving her legs further apart with his knees.

"What do you say, witch?" he whispered, as he nudged himself gentle against her, just dipping the swollen painted head of him into her wet, mouthwatering heat. "Will you beg your lord, your master, your affianced *husband*, for his dick?"

Kay's moan was guttural and thrilling, her breasts heaving beneath him, her eyes staring at him with something straddling shock and craving and reverence. "Yes," she gasped, the single word a streak of glorious heat, straight to Mik's already-straining cock. "Yes, please, master, my lord, my—my *husband*, please, *fuck* me."

Fuck, yes. And with a harsh, triumphant, desperate howl, Mik plunged himself deep inside. Carving through his witch's wet heat straight to the core of her, while she screamed beneath him, her body and her hands clamping tight around him, trapping him, clinging to him, hers.

"Oh gods," she gasped, her voice breaking, as Mik dragged

himself out, slow, watching her, revelling in her. "Oh gods, Mik, oh gods, oh—"

Her voice flared into another scream as he drove home again, hard and frantic and desperate, and suddenly he couldn't control it, couldn't stop it, couldn't think. Only had to take her, batter her, break her like she'd broken him, prove himself as her lord and master and ogre and husband, show himself worthy of his goddess witch wife. Taking it, giving it, in flesh and promise and pain, in sickness and health, in the screaming gift of her body and his own furious driving onslaught. Building and building and building, until—

His release poured out of him in a flood, in wave after wave of crashing, raging pleasure. Pounding her, filling her with his surging spraying seed, hammering home his words with actions and truth and power. With the promise of new life, planted with purpose deep under his promised wife's skin.

When the world slowly turned aright again, it was with Mik's body still inside Kay's, his forehead to hers, their breaths gasping as one. And with wet faces, whether his or hers, Mik didn't care, and he kissed away the tears on her skin, tasting salt in his mouth, streaking paint on her smooth cheek.

"You're sure, love?" his hoarse voice said. "Because we could still rush you off to a healer, before anything goes too far."

But Kay was still clinging to him, as if to trap him there, her hand sinking wide into the sticky-feeling mess of his hair. "I'm sure," her shaky voice replied. "But are *you*?"

Mik pulled up a little, so he could look at her, make her see the truth in his eyes. "Yes," he said. "I am, Kay. I love you."

She gave an odd, lurching little gasp, her eyes leaking again at the corners, her body under him and around him giving a hard, sustained shiver. "But I," she began, and now her other hand was here, tracing light and stinging against what had to be a fresh cut, on his cheek. "I *hurt* you, Mik, I don't know what came over me, I just completely lost it, I'm so, so sorry."

Her voice threatened to break again, but Mik brushed her ridiculous apologies away with a shake of his head, an amused quirk of his mouth. "I deserved it," he said. "I know you've have stopped if I asked. And honestly"—he raised his brows—"if you'd gone any easier on me, I'd have been disappointed. A lord has to have *some* standards, witch."

Kay choked a laugh, her hand in his hair tightening against his scalp. "What standards?" she asked. "You just proposed to your *housemaid*, Mik."

Her voice sounded teasing, but her eyes were decidedly not, and Mik pulled up further onto his elbows, looked down at her. "You're not my housemaid," he said firmly. "You were never just my housemaid. You're my best friend, who's a brilliant artist, and a brilliant earth-mage. And you'll be a brilliant lord's wife, too."

Kay gave another hard shiver beneath him, but her eyes darted another brief, betraying glance to the side. To her new little cottage, her new life, and Mik followed her gaze, looked past the mess they'd made, to the place she'd made her home.

"We'll work it out," he said, and he meant that. "You should keep this place, keep on living here if you want. We can wait on the wedding, give you some time to establish yourself first, give some time between you being my employee and my wife. And maybe time to change your mind, too, if you want."

But Kay's blonde head was shaking beneath him, hard, her eyes back to almost reverent on his. "Not going to change my mind," she whispered. "Not *ever*, Mik."

The relief filtered across Mik's body, across his mouth, and he smiled down at her, warm and affectionate. "You sure?" he asked. "What happens if I decide that you need to accompany me on any and all visits to my tenants? And sit in on my endless meetings with Scullen, and go shopping with Lea in my stead? And spar and train with me, and teach me how to improve my air-shields, and, most importantly"—he took a breath—"keep your lord properly fucked and humbled, whenever I need it?"

He'd meant it to sound lighthearted, but it hadn't quite come out that way, and he felt his eyes searching, watchful, on hers. "Would you?" he asked, quieter. "Even before the wedding? I know all that would take you away from your work here, but—"

But I need you, he wanted to say, and bit the words off just in time. But maybe he hadn't needed to, because Kay was finally smiling back up at him, slow and stunning, her eyes alight. Transforming her once again into his goddess, streaked and spattered and sated on the floor beneath him.

"Of course I would," she said, quiet and fervent. "You're still my best friend too, Mik. And I would *like* doing all those things. And, also, if you think I would ever allow my betrothed lord husband to swan about like an arrogant prat"—her smile twitched at the corner, turned into something else—"then your tight little lordly arse is going to get a *very* rude awakening."

Mik laughed out loud, his eyes crinkling, his gut giving a satisfied little lurch at the responding flare of heat in Kay's eyes. "Don't look now, witch," he replied, "but my lordly arse is already being very rudely awakened. By a fucking filthy *paint brush*, at that."

He could see the sudden shock on Kay's face, her head abruptly craning up to look behind him—where indeed, her paintbrush was still lodged inside him, jutting up out between his arse-cheeks. And though she laughed, too, that heat was still rising in her eyes, and Mik could feel that paintbrush give a sudden, gut-swarming little dip, twisting its way further inside him.

"Witch," he hissed, but the pleasure was already flaring, both behind his eyes, and in his twitching dick, still safely encased in her hot dark heat. "You're going to *pay* for that."

But she only smiled, so warm and raw and breathtaking, his

beautiful Kay. Winding her arms and legs up around him, and looking at him as though he was her lord, her god, her love, her salvation.

"As you wish, my lord," she said. "I am forever at your service."

THE END

THANKS FOR READING!

Thank you so much for joining me for Mik and Kay's story!

This novella was originally inspired by my research into historical titled men, and how they often behaved with their household staff. It isn't an easy topic to read about, and I ended up wanting to write my own version of it—one where the lord is properly humbled, and learns a few important lessons!

If you'd like to read about more arrogant air-mages being humbled, the next book in this series is *The Mage's Match*, and it's about Mik's friend Regin Agmund. The realm's most famous celebrity has lost his magic, and no one can bring it back... except for a poor, unfashionable commoner.

I also have a free Mages story for members of my mailing list! In *The Mage's Groom*, a haughty mage has been misbehaving, and now she's about to get the correction she deserves. Find it at finleyfenn.com.

Finally, if you enjoyed this book, I hope you'll share your thoughts! I'm always so, so grateful when readers leave reviews on my books, but I'd also love to hear your feedback on my Facebook group, Discord server, or Patreon. You can find them all linked on my website at finleyfenn.com.

Thank you again for joining me for this tale! Hugs!

ACKNOWLEDGMENTS

Once again, I'm so thankful for all the readers and friends who have shared their enthusiasm and support for this series. It means so much to me!

I also want to mention the awesome beta readers who have offered me their insights on this book: Anne-Marie, Jo Henny Wolf, and Lauren Mauchley. I'm also deeply grateful to my proofreader Emmy at Bra Bedre Belt, and to my incredible author friends who have so kindly supported this book.

I'm also forever thankful to my generous Patreon supporters, my advance reviewers, my Skai Librarian Amy, and my steadfast Right Hand Marykate.

And of course, my deepest gratitude to my own magical husband, who has always given me all his faithfulness and support. Thank you, my love.

NEXT IN THE MAGES SERIES

THE MAGE'S MATCH
The Mages: Book 1

The world's greatest air-mage has lost his magic. And only she can bring it back...

Once, Regin Agmund was the realm's greatest lightning-caster—rich, famous, arrogant, and deadly.

Until he lost his magic.

Even the best experts can't understand it, and Regin is furious, miserable, and desperate enough to do anything... or anyone.

Even if it's a poor, unfashionable commoner...

Selby Seng is a simple, plainspoken pedlar, who practices an illicit branch of earth-magic.

She's shocked when she's confronted with an astonishing claim: **she has a deep magical affinity with the great Regin Agmund.** An affinity strong enough to bring his magic back.

The catch? Affinities work through closeness. Proximity. *Touch.*

It means moving in with the realm's richest, most notorious celebrity, and serving his every whim.

Even if he hates her. Even if he's cold and selfish and cruel. Even if he can barely look at her while he's taking his due...

But in Regin Agmund's volatile world of power, privilege, and danger, maybe an honest, grounded pedlar is just what he desperately needs...

Unless he destroys her first.

ALSO BY FINLEY FENN

THE MAGE'S GROOM
The Mages: Bonus Story
with Email Signup

When a brilliant mage gives up and goes home, she finds her master waiting...

Greta Hendersson was supposed to do great things in life. Build a career, rack up accolades, make a perfect marriage.

But when her two-year relationship with the world's most famous air-mage blows up in her face, everything else falls apart, too. And all that's left is to go home...

To where her head groom has been patiently waiting. **With a collar and whip in his hand...**

FREE download!
www.finleyfenn.com

ALSO BY FINLEY FENN

THE MAGE'S MASTER
The Mages: Book 2

She's a rich, haughty heiress. And he's about to make her pay...

Fasta Valgeirr always gets what she wants. She's rich, poised, and beautiful, and one of the top earth-mages in the realm.

But she can't have the one thing she wants most: Henrik Hallen. **Her poor, working-class employee.**

Henrik is big, burly, and commanding, crushing rocks and hurling boulders with dizzying power. And though Fasta's often caught his yearning glances toward her, he's always kept their relationship friendly. Respectful. Professional.

Until Henrik lands in deep trouble. And Fasta is waiting and ready to help, with one condition...

Henrik finally gives her what she wants. And in return, he can indulge his own forbidden fantasies, too...

But Henrik's longings are even darker than Fasta imagined. And he won't stand for a casual, throwaway affair with his spoiled, entitled boss.

Instead, he wants to put Fasta in her place in the dirt. Teach her who's really in charge. And give her a humbling she'll never forget...

Can Fasta bend the knee to her rough, dangerous new ruler, and learn her lesson? **Or will she end up forever crushed?**

ALSO BY FINLEY FENN

THE LADY AND THE ORC

He's the most feared monster in the realm. And she's what he needs to win his war...

In a world of warring orcs and men, Lady Norr is condemned to a childless marriage, a cruel lord husband, and a life of genteel poverty—until the day her home is ransacked by a horde. And leading the charge is their hulking, deadly orc captain: the infamous Grimarr.

And Grimarr has a wicked plan for Lady Norr, and for ending this war once and for all. She's going to become his captive—and the perfect snare for Lord Norr.

There's no possible escape, and soon Lady Norr is dragged off toward Orc Mountain in the powerful arms of her greatest enemy. A ruthless, commanding warlord, with a velvet voice and mouthwatering scent, who awakens every forbidden hunger she never knew she had...

But Grimarr refuses to accept half measures—in war, or in pleasure. And before he'll conquer Lady Norr's deepest, darkest desires, she needs to surrender *everything*.

Her allegiance.

Her wedding ring.

Her future...

And with her husband's forces giving chase, Lady Norr can't afford to play such a dangerous game—or can she? **Even if this deadly orc's plans might be the only way to save them all?**

ABOUT THE AUTHOR

Finley Fenn is "the queen of dark orc romance" (Virgo Reader), and her ongoing Orc Sworn series has been praised as "sexy, romantic, angsty, and captivating ... utter brilliance" (Romantically Inclined Reviews).

When she's not obsessing over her stories, Finley loves reading, drooling over delicious orc artwork, and spending time with her incredible readers on Patreon, Discord, and Facebook. She lives in Canada with her beloved family, including her very own grumpy, gorgeous husband.

For free bonus stories and epilogues, special offers, and exclusive Orc Sworn artwork, sign up at www.finleyfenn.com.